# THE
# MONEY
# RULE

JOHNNY MEE

Copyright © 2017 Johnny Mee

www.johnnynovels.com

*Cover by The Innocent Bystanders and based on the original design by Andy Gutowski of 423 Creative*

ISBN: 1981456244
ISBN-13: 978-1981456246

# OTHER BILLY MACK THRILLERS:

## THE PERSIAN WALTZ
*Volume 1 - Rome*

## THE OTHER RULE
*Volume 2 - London*

## THE CARDINAL RULE
*Volume 3 – Rome*

## THE SWEETEST PAYBACK
*Volume 4 – Barcelona*

# ACKNOWLEDGMENTS

## THANK YOU

**Caroline Ciaglia** (again!) for your help, your superb advice and your keen eye -- all treasured.

**Chris Kozak** for your assistance and advice with marketing.

**Monroe DeVos** and **Liz Scott** for your help with the cover art.

**Peter Weum** for your assistance with the manuscript.

# DEDICATION

To Rainer, Bettina, Henri and Anna Dobianer.
Your friendship is invaluable!

# CHAPTER 1

Billy Mack inspected the dazzling array of Swiss watches spread out in the store window display and noticed the time on each watch was exactly the same, down to the second. *Only in Switzerland*, he thought. The time on each watch gave him five more minutes before he met Siva and they began their vacation.

His eyes came back to the Rolex with a price tag of $77,000. "That costs more than my car," he said under his breath. Then he added, a little louder this time, "Who would pay that for a watch?"

A heavy-set man with a salt and pepper beard standing to Mack's left chortled then replied with a heavy German accent, "A man with too much money."

Mack looked the man in the eye and was about to reply when the man's expression turned serious. He held out a business card and said, "Give this to Siva. She's expecting it. She is to call the number on back as soon as her business is completed."

Mack took the card then flinched when a young woman, inside the display window, reached down and removed the expensive Rolex. She glanced up through the window and shot Mack a patronizing grin. She turned and walked away, her white-gloved hands carefully cradling the Rolex.

Acting as if his reaction was normal, Mack swept back his thick brown hair and stood up straight, his eyes still following the woman.

When she disappeared he gathered himself and studied the card. Printed in block letters was: *Herr Schmidt*. He turned it over and read the back. He flipped the card back over then lifted his head and looked to his left and then to his right. The heavy-set man was gone.

He brought his eyes back down to the card as if it would tell him where the man went. There only a name on the front and a number on the back.

He put the card in his shirt pocket while he scanned the area hoping to spot the man. He slowly spun three-sixty and studied the crowded street.

A minute later, he strolled across the street, stepped over a set of tram tracks and entered *Paradeplatz*. He stood in the center of the small city square and did another three-sixty looking for the man. The square was the heart of Zürich's financial center and the address of all the top Swiss banks.

Quitting time was approaching and the streets were steadily filling with bankers wearing either bespoke suits or designer dresses. Walking through *Paradeplatz* he peered up at the impressive stone buildings. There was more money on deposit in the banks headquartered in the square mile around him than anywhere else in the world. He wondered if *Zürich* was the German word for money.

He walked across the square and waited for a blue tram to pass. The tram's destination was written above the driver: *TIEFENBRUNNEN*. After the crowded tram passed, Mack checked the tracks in both directions and stepped off the curb.

He crossed the street then walked a half block, turned left and strolled down a narrow cobblestone side street. Straight ahead of him, at the end of the short street, was the broadside of a long, salmon-colored building. All three floors had large windows spaced every ten feet. The shutters were closed on every window except for the center window on the second floor. Inside the window, a man leaned against the window ledge reading something in his hand.

The salmon-colored building had a pitched roof with wooden shingles. The freshly painted building looked out of place among the taller stone-block structures hovering over it. It looked more like a tool shed for the surrounding buildings than a place of work.

Little did anyone know this tranquil old building had the tightest security in Zürich, in all of Switzerland.

It was the headquarters of Keller Bank, the most exclusive private bank in the world. This sedate, ordinary building was where the world's wealthiest hid their money. It was well known among the rich that Keller only took on clients willing and able to deposit a minimum of $100 million.

Mack turned the corner and headed toward the bank's front entrance. He stopped in his tracks as Siva Afari burst through the bank's thick glass doors, her black hair flowing behind her. She wore black pants, a sheer white blouse and a black leather biker's jacket with **DUCATI** written across the front in red letters. Her demeanor said something was wrong. Siva's face was mixture of unrestrained anger and contempt. Mack rarely saw her this upset.

Hustling out the door behind her was a short,

bald man in a gray suit and brown shoes. He was barking at her as he closed the gap between them.

Siva abruptly stopped. She kept her back to the man and impatiently tapped her foot.

The bald man stood next to her and said something while his head bobbed up and down. It was obvious he didn't want to face her.

Siva cut him off and slowly turned. Her jaw was clenched as she spoke sternly, wagging her finger in his face like he was a disobedient child.

The man closed his eyes and slowly rattled his head as if he disagreed with her.

When Siva finished talking, the bald man frowned then shrugged his shoulders and stuck out his hand. Mack read the man's lips: *"I'm very sorry."*

Siva slapped the man's hand away and marched toward Mack with the look of anger and contempt back on her face.

Mack stepped back around the corner and waited. Siva marched up, grabbed him by the elbow and dragged him down a narrow passageway, out of sight from the bank's front door and the banker.

She spun Mack so they were face to face. "Can you believe what that jackass just told me?"

"Not until you tell me," Mack replied as casually

as he knew how.

Siva looked at Mack like he was a smart ass. In her state, it took her a second to realize Mack didn't know what just happened. She closed her eyes and sucked in a deep breath to calm down.

"The account I opened for a *mutual friend* has been emptied." The way she pronounced *mutual friend* made if obvious there was no friendship involved. "Every penny is gone."

Mack chewed on his words as he thought through the questions piling up in his mind.

He realized he better say something. "Maybe your mutual friend transferred the money and hasn't yet told you."

Siva squeezed Mack's elbow and said, "He doesn't have the access codes. Only I do."

Mack massaged his chin with his free hand. "Where did the money go? That may tell us something."

"Nobody at the bank would tell me. In fact, I was repeatedly told they *couldn't* tell me because they didn't know."

Mack glanced back. The bald banker had wandered around the corner and stood in plain view, staring at Mack and Siva with his phone in his ear.

He caught eyes with Mack and nodded his head as he spoke into his phone. He turned the phone around and snapped a picture.

"What's the banker's name?" Mack asked. "He just took a picture of us."

Siva thought for a second. "Gullberg, Marek Gullberg."

Mack glared at Gullberg and shook his head letting Gullberg know there would be no more pictures.

Gullberg got the message, shoved his phone in his pocket and walked back to the bank's entrance.

Mack took Siva by the elbow and said, "Let's go someplace quiet and talk. Someplace out of the way."

They hurried out to the street, crossed the tram tracks and strolled across *Paradeplatz*. They skirted the crowd as they marched past a waiting tram. A block past the plaza they turned and walked down a small set of steps to a footpath running along a canal. Motorboats were docked in one continuous line along the footpath, all covered with the same blue tarp. Fifty meters later they came to a footbridge and crossed the canal.

In the middle of the next block was a small café with a raised deck running along the side of the building. It was a rare sunny day in Zürich and all the outdoor tables were occupied.

Mack checked inside and found every table empty. "We can talk in here," he said. He led Siva to a table against the back wall. Mack sat and faced the door.

Neither said a word until the waitress took their order then made her way outside.

Siva leaned across the table. "There was a hundred million dollars in that account," she whispered as if she were afraid to even say it. She sat back and loudly added, "A hundred million."

Her breathing became erratic and she rubbed her hands together as if she was trying to dry them.

Mack realized Siva was about to go into panic mode. He had to make sure she kept her wits about her. He calmly lifted his hands and said, "Before we determine what to do, we figure out a few things. First, why the bank transferred the money without your approval, your access codes, or even your knowledge."

Siva slumped back in her chair.

Mack pulled Herr Schmidt's card from his shirt pocket and slid it across the table. "I was instructed to give you this. You were asked to call the number on back once your business was completed."

Siva read the name on the card then flipped the card over. After a second, she asked, "When did you get this?"

"It was given to me ten minutes ago." Mack answered, looking past Siva as he spoke.

Siva furrowed her brow, tilted her head and gave Mack a puzzled look.

"While I waited for you, I was window shopping when this guy handed me that card and said, 'Give this to your friend Siva and have her to call the number on back when her business is completed.' Then he disappeared into thin air."

Siva kept her eyes on the card and released some tension in her jaw. "I was told somebody would contact me at the appropriate time."

Mack tapped the card with is his finger. "Who is Herr Schmidt?"

"I don't know. I was told that after I transferred money someone would contact me with contact information and instructions to be given to the recipient of that transfer. But... I wasn't able to make the transfer." Siva turned the card over and re-read the phone number printed on the back. "This is a local number, a cell phone number... probably untraceable. If I call him, what do I say?"

Mack wasn't looking at Siva as she spoke. His

eyes were concentrating on the sidewalk outside.

"Are you listening to me?" She said curtly.

Mack slapped twenty Swiss francs on the table as he looked around the café. He grabbed Siva by the hand and said, "Let's go." He ushered her behind the café counter to the kitchen door and pushed his way through.

"You're hurting my hand, Billy," Siva said as they crossed the small kitchen.

Mack relaxed his grip but did not let go.

"What's going on? Why are you in such a hurry?"

"The same person has walked past the café three times."

$

# CHAPTER 2

Mack kicked open the back door of the kitchen and pulled Siva out into an asphalt courtyard surrounded by five-story buildings. Dumpsters and recycling bins were scattered around the square. In the middle of the square, two rows of cars glistened brightly from the sun reflecting off the upper windows.

Mack squinted as he peered around. "This way," he said.

Siva pulled her hand away and shook it.

Mack looked at her strangely.

"We'll move faster this way," she said.

Mack was a step ahead of Siva as they crossed the courtyard heading to a tunnel wide enough for only one car. He scrutinized the street at the other end of the tunnel then jogged through. Siva walked briskly after him.

Mack stepped out on the street and flagged a taxi. He opened the back door and held it for Siva. She jumped in and he followed, slamming the door behind him.

"Opera House and hurry," he said to the taxi driver.

"Why the Opera House?" Siva asked.

"There are always crowds in and around it. If someone is following us, we can hide in plain site."

The taxicab jerked forward, throwing Mack and Siva back against the seat. The driver barely slowed as he approached an intersection.

"Did you forget your friend?" The taxi driver asked, pointing behind him with his thumb.

Mack turned in his seat to see the man he recognized as going back and forth in front of the café. "No, maybe he wanted this taxi?"

"If you say so."

The taxi driver turned right and drove along the Sihl River until he reached Lake Zürich. After turning left, he looked at Mack in the rearview mirror and said, "I can only take you close to the Opera House. There is construction blocking the roads. I can take you around the construction and drop you at the building next door. Is that okay?"

"That would be fine, thank you." Siva answered.

As they drove along the lake, Mack and Siva quietly peered out the window looking for what shouldn't be there.

The taxi drove past the Opera House, snaked through road construction zones and approached the Opera House from the opposite direction. The driver turned his head and looked at Mack. "I believe we are being followed. The same car has been three spaces behind since we reached Lake Zürich. What do you want me to do?"

"Find a spot where only one car can stop and we will jump out." He tossed a hundred Swiss franc note onto the driver's lap. "This should more than cover your fare."

"Thank you very much, sir. I will drop you by the Brasserie. You know the Brasserie, yes?"

"Yes, that works."

The taxi sped up. At the next intersection the driver ran a red light. With a huge grin on his face, he said, "That will help us."

Outside the Brasserie, the driver slammed on the brakes, skidding to a stop. "Hurry," he said. "If you need, you can go through the Brasserie. There is an exit on the far side."

Mack jumped out, helped Siva step out then leaned into the car and handed the driver another hundred Swiss francs. "You never saw us," he said and slammed the car door.

He and Siva jogged up the steps and into the Brasserie. It was late afternoon and the bar was empty except for a young couple at the far end of the bar embraced in a passionate kiss, oblivious to anything going on around them.

Mack and Siva walked to the bar and positioned themselves so they could see the traffic out on the street.

"Keep an eye out for cars stopping out front and I'll watch the entrance," Mack said.

The bartender approached and Mack waved him away. "We haven't decided yet," he said in German.

Five minutes passed in nervous silence. Siva's hands were shaking. She interlaced her fingers and said, "I'm scared, Billy. The people who entrusted me with that money won't be happy when they learn their money is gone."

Billy stroked Siva's forearm. "It's too early to panic. You don't know what happened yet. A hundred million doesn't just disappear."

"After that meeting at Keller Bank, I have a real bad feeling. I don't know what to do. I need your help to figure this out."

Mack was surprised she felt like she had to ask for his help. "Of course. Tell me what happened and don't leave anything out. Even the smallest detail may mean something. Start at the beginning, from the time you agreed to open the account."

Mack kept a watchful eye on the front door as Siva collected her thoughts.


A minute later, she said, "A few months ago, I was at home in Vienna when Ray Gunn called. He said a former colleague would be visiting me to discuss an important arrangement." Siva flicked up her eyebrows when she said *arrangement*. "Ray didn't elaborate but asked me to hear his colleague out. Two days later, I was having a coffee at a small café when a man sat down at my table. He introduced himself as Herr Huber, Ray Gunn's colleague. He asked me to take a walk. We strolled over to the nearby park and he proceeded to tell me he needed me open an account at Keller Bank in Zürich to front wire transfers to numbered accounts located in banks in Liechtenstein, Malta and Cyprus. I would receive the wire transfer instructions along with a plane ticket to Zürich. On a specific date, I was to make the transfers and follow up with specific instructions. That's when I asked him why he trusted me."

Mack cut her off and said, "Because Ray Gunn recommended you, right?"

Siva nodded. "He said Ray was one of a handful of people he trusted and if Ray trusted me that was good enough for him. When I didn't react, Herr Huber went on. I was to be the sole name on the account and be the only person who could direct the bank on what to do with the money."

"Let's jump ahead. It's obvious you agreed."

"Only after I said I had to speak with Ray before I gave him my answer."

"What did Ray say?"

Siva pressed her lips together as she contemplated her words.

Mack's hand shot up to keep Siva from saying anything.

"Shit," he said. "The man who kept walking past

the café earlier just came into the bar."

A muscular man in a tweed sport coat, blue jeans and black lace up boots strode through the door with a smirk on his face. He marched up to Mack and Siva with his right hand in his coat pocket.

"Ms. Afari, please come with me."

It was not a request.

"She's not going anywhere until you tell us who you are and why you've been following us," Mack replied while trying to figure out what kind of weapon the man was carrying.

"This doesn't involve you."

"What are you going to do, shoot me?"

The man looked slowly around the bar then removed his hand from his pocket. His fingers gripped a Glock 9 with a short suppressor attached to the barrel. "This makes just enough noise for me to have to kill everyone in this bar and I don't really want to do that. I count four people who would die, you, the bartender and that annoying couple at the other end of the bar tongue wrestling." He pointed the gun at Mack's chest. "You'll be first."

"Tell me why," Siva said.

"My employer has questions for you. That's all you need to know."

"If you want me to leave here with you, Billy comes along."

The man gave Mack a quizzical look. "You're Billy Mack?"

Mack didn't answer him.

"I thought I recognized you. I grew up in Chicago and was Sox fan." The man thought for a second then said, "He can come along only if he keeps his mouth shut."

"Lead the way," Mack said.

"Yeah right," the man said with a chuckle. "I'll be a step behind you." He flicked the barrel of the gun toward the door. "You were very fast when you played baseball Mr. Billy Mack but even then you couldn't outrun a bullet. Don't do anything stupid."

Mack took Siva by the hand and walked to the door. At the top of the steps, Mack felt the man close on his heels.

Mack and Siva took the first step down when Mack felt a swoosh zip past his ear. He heard a wet thump over his shoulder and spun around. The man behind him was falling back with a large hole in the center of his forehead. Blood spatter covered the front door and the side window.

The man lay sprawled out on the top step. His

legs reflexively twitched as blood pooled around his head and began trickling down the steps.

A woman at the bottom of the stairs let out an ear-shattering scream then bent over and threw up.

Mack tried to remember if he'd heard a gun shot. He was sure he hadn't. Mack stopped thinking, grabbed Siva by the arm and hustled her down the steps onto the crowded sidewalk.

"Keep walking and don't look back. Act as though nothing has happened."

$

# CHAPTER 3

Beat *(pronounced 'Bay-Ott')* Keller was President and Chief Executive Officer of Keller Bank, the world's most exclusive private bank. The bank managed, invested and hid the money of the world's wealthiest. To become a client of Keller Bank you had to be referred to Keller personally by a current bank client, pass an extensive background check, sign a strict non-disclosure agreement and finally, deposit a minimum of $100 million.

There was another side of Keller Bank known only to a small, select group of people. Keller Bank was the covert banker to the world's most powerful intelligence agencies. If and when discreet payments were required, Keller Bank was utilized because of their ability to keep the anonymity of the agencies involved.

Beat Keller founded the bank twenty-five years ago and built it into the juggernaut of Swiss private banking. He owned eighty percent of the bank. The other twenty percent was owned by Keller's two ex-wives, stakes they received from their pre-nuptial agreements. The only stipulation Keller put on his ex-wives was a strict non-disclosure of how much of Keller Bank's profit they received. If this information became public, for any reason, both ex-wives forfeited their ownership. For millions of good reasons, both ex-wives guarded that information with their lives.

Keller was soft in the middle from years of French wine, Swiss cheese and Cuban cigars. He worked twelve hours a day and, at the end of the day, counted his money. For one hour each day, he needed to escape, to relax, reflect and recharge. Unless the world was ending, he was not to be disturbed during this hour, his hour.

Every afternoon from 3:55 to 4:55, Keller meditated in his private *Relaxation Grotto*, a seven million dollar chamber one floor below his large office. The temperature in the room was kept exactly at seventy-two degrees. The room was acoustically perfect and the chaise lounges were designed specifically for Keller's body. Relaxing sounds, such as a rain forest or a babbling brook, pumped softly through hidden speakers. Water crawled down the muted gold and silver-flaked walls providing a soothing affect on the senses. At exactly 4:45 every day, Keller rose from one of his lounge chairs, strolled over to the corner shower and let a warm waterfall pour over him for exactly 5 minutes. A hot air blower then dried him off. At 4:55, he was back in his office ready for four more hours of work before dinner at one of Zürich's top restaurants.

Mercedes Geissel burst through the Relaxation Grotto's door and hurried across the tile floor, her high heels clicking loudly as she ran. It was 4:25, interrupting Keller's meditation.

Geissel was the bank's Chief Operating Officer. She was promoted to that position six months ago.

She was five-feet four inches tall with brown hair and dark brown eyes. She wore a navy blazer, blue blouse and gray slacks, her uniform.

She marched up to Keller lying naked in his lounge chair, averted her eyes and cleared her throat.

Keller haltingly opened his eyes. "This better be important, Mercy" he said through clenched teeth.

"I am very sorry to bother you but we have a

major problem." Geissel waited for Keller to respond.

He just glared at her.

Unable to endure his hard stare any longer, she sat on the lounge chair next to him. She hesitantly turned and faced him.

Keller twisted his head, his eyes still holding his hard stare. "Spit it out Mercy. I don't pay you to stare at me."

Geissel swallowed hard. "There is a hundred million dollars missing from a new account. The client is livid and demanding the money be immediately returned."

Keller fought to remain calm. "Who's the client?"

"Siva Afari," Geissel answered then bit her lip hoping Keller knew Afari and would offer to step in and handle the situation.

"Refresh my memory," Keller said as he sat up and grabbed his white terry cloth robe off the floor. He threw on the robe then stood over Geissel.

Geissel said, "She is one of our double D clients." Double D was the bank's internal reference for *'Distinctive and Discreet'* accounts owned by select intelligence services. "The hundred million was sitting in cash as required by those clients."

"Who's the rich uncle this time?"

"The wire transfer trail, or trails, indicate two of them, the Americans and the Israelis. Afari has a history with both."

"The Israelis? Damn. They don't play nice when shit like this happens." Keller fought to keep his composure.

"It's the Americans I'm worried about," Geissel countered. "When Afari left our offices, she met an American, someone we've never dealt with before. He was sly enough to stay away from our security cameras but we have a photo of him. We ran our facial recognition programs and learned his name is William A. McMillan but everyone calls him Billy Mack. I have our security team digging up everything they can on him to find out which agency he works for or if he's a freelancer."

"If he's a pro, how did he let you take a photo?"

"When he met Afari, Marek Gullberg was able to covertly take a picture with his phone."

"I thought Gullberg resigned to join another bank?"

"He did but his contract requires him to give thirty days notice. He's the operations manager for the Double D accounts and is still responsible for those accounts."

"Call security and walk Gullberg out of the bank. Have his personal belongings sent to him, after you carefully go through everything."

"Of course. What about this Billy Mack?"

"Get me the background on him. I will then make discreet inquiries to a few high level sources."

Geissel stood to leave.

"Sit your ass back down," Keller barked. "Tell me how the money went missing."

"We don't know what happened to the money. The transfer followed protocol but Ms. Afari is adamant she didn't authorize any wire transfers."

Keller's eyes widened and his breathing intensified. "How in the hell... What the..." He caught his stutter, sniffed and said, "We have the greatest system and cyber security in existence. Are you telling me someone breached out system?"

"No, of course not but Afari is insistent that we transferred the money without her knowledge. I'm working on finding out if that's true, which I doubt. Everything else has taken a back seat."

"Where's Khandelwal on this?" Lee Khandelwal was the bank's Chief Technology Officer and the world's leading expert on cyber security.

"He should be in his office by now. He just returned from the Ukraine where he installed our security system for our newest client in Kiev. I thought it prudent not to say anything to him until I spoke with you."

Keller cinched his robe tighter. "Tell Lee I want him in my office in ten minutes. Ms. Afari could cause problems if she's running a scam. If she's not, we have an internal disaster, a major failure. Either way, get to the bottom of this fast. Have the security team run full checks on every employee to see if there are any connections to Afari or Mack. If someone's in bed with them, we bring the hammer down."

"Let me bring in Bella. She works fast and will have the money back before word gets out. If we bring in the security team, we run the risk of exposure, loose lips and all. The last thing we want is for our competitors to find out." Geissel said. "Besides, Double D clients have the unique ability to manipulate systems, including ours. It's obvious Afari and her accomplice, this Billy Mack, are behind this. Bella can separate them by getting Mack out of the picture. With Mack dead, Afari will know her only option is to return the money."

"Bella will need time to get up to speed. Khandelwal and his people can solve this faster. He can also have his people review each and every account."

"I checked and no other accounts were affected."

"Not yet. If Afari is telling the truth we have to move fast. Who has access to Afari's account?"

"Only Afari, she set up the account and provided the required security measures. She claims she didn't provide her account information to anyone."

"How well do we know Afari?"

"She's had other accounts with us. The last one was closed three years ago. We have a file on her but it's thin. She's a tool used to front Double D accounts. That tells me Mack is the brains behind the stolen money."

"Have it and Billy Mack's file to me before I talk to Khandelwal."

"We don't have a file on Billy Mack but are compiling one as we speak. I will have both Mack and Afari's files to you as soon as Mack's is completed. In the meantime, I urge you to bring in Bella and let her have a go at Mack. This is a job for a pro."

Keller untied his robe, dropped it on the floor then strolled over to the waterfall shower in the corner. He said over his shoulder, "Not yet. Let's see what Khandelwal and his team can do first."

Geissel scurried after him. "We should bring her in now. The longer we wait, the less the chance we have of recovering the money. She's never failed us."

"She shoots first and asks questions later. I'll give our technology expert a chance to investigate. Let's see if Khandelwal is as good as his reputation. I will give him twenty-four hours then we can discuss using Bella."

"Yes sir."

Keller glared on Geissel. "The reason I promoted you was because you proved you could bring in the big fish, the whales. You brought in the Sunden General Partners' $500 million account and I approved it based on your personal recommendation. You then landed big whales from Eastern Europe when your predecessor failed and you seamlessly closed the Afari Double D account. You were a star." Keller shot Geissel a look of disgust. "Do I now have a major problem with your accounts?"

"No, of course not. I will do whatever's necessary to fix this."

"I groomed you since you were fourteen to run my bank." Keller said.

Groomed? Geissel thought. She looked at Keller

with jaded eyes. Is that what you're calling it now — groomed?

Keller had seen that look many times before. "I took you and your sister in when your parents died and did everything to make your lives better," Keller said.

"My parents were murdered," Geissel replied coldly.

Keller ignored her, stepped under the waterfall shower and looked over his shoulder. "Don't disappoint me."

"I won't disappoint." Geissel turned to leave. "I won't disappoint... myself," she mumbled.

Keller clamped his eyes shut and screamed, "Find the money and the assholes responsible. Nobody steals from Beat Keller... nobody."

"Then let me bring in Bella and get this over with," Geissel begged.

"Let me think about that. While I'm thinking, get Bella up to speed so she can hit the ground running if and only if I need her."

$

# CHAPTER 4

Mack and Siva hastened their pace away from the dead man lying in the doorway. A chorus of police sirens was closing in on the Brasserie.

Mack stopped for a second to get his bearings. Being out in the open and unprotected unnerved him. He surveyed the surroundings for anyone paying attention to him or Siva.

Siva pulled him into *Sechseläutentplatz*, a large open square in front the Brasserie and Opera House. The square was bigger than two football fields.

They zigzagged their way through the swarm of commuters coming at them. Most of the crowd was coming from the Bellevue tram station and heading across the square to *Stadlehofen*, Zürich second largest train station, for the final leg of their commute home.

Mack and Siva stayed close to on-coming people, brushing past them without slowing down, using the crowd as cover.

At the Bellevue tram station, Mack pointed up the hill to *Niederdorf*, the name for Zürich's old town section. "Up that way."

They crossed a busy intersection against the light. Local Swiss stopped and stared at them in amazement, their mouths agape. Some people pointed at them like they'd just mugged someone. In Zürich, only common criminals cross against the light.

As they headed up the hill, Mack pulled out his phone, tapped the screen and brought it to his ear.

"Hi Cici, is he in?"

"Hi Billy, let me check."

A minute later, Cici came back on the line. "Yes, Ray's in but he can't talk right now. He wants you to go straight to Peter and he'll call you there."

"How did he know?" Mack asked.

"He'll call you there," Cici said and hung up.

Mack checked the streets signs. They were standing at the intersection of *Münstergasse*, the main pedestrian street in the old town, and *Spiegelgasse*. "Ray gave me a name and address, just in case. We'll be there in ten minutes," he said in a comforting tone.

Mack shoved the phone back in his pocket and peered up the street. "Let's walk and talk."

They strolled up *Spiegelgasse,* a narrow, winding alley as if they were out for a leisurely walk. When they were out of sight of *Münstergasse*, Siva stopped and faced Mack.

"We were almost killed back there, Billy. That wasn't what I signed up for."

Mack put his hands on Siva's shoulders and gave her a reassuring squeeze, just strong enough not to rattle her. He waited for her to look him in the eye and said, "If whoever took that shot wanted us dead, we wouldn't be having this conversation."

"You don't know that."

Mack eased his grip then pulled his hands from Siva's shoulders. He soberly massaged his chin, a habit he was trying to break. "This city is a hotbed for spies, swindlers, and the miscreants that feed off them. It's been that way since the end of World War II. Spies only kill as a last resort. If the dead man is from the wrong country, the Swiss will turn a blind eye."

She didn't believe Mack. "The Swiss are neutral."

"Neutrality has nothing to do with it. The business of Zürich is money, no questions asked. The city lives by the money rule. You have money, you rule. Two things spies like, power and money."

"I thought spies demanded secrecy?"

"In Zürich, money talks but never says a word."

"What does that have to do with our situation?"

"Spies and swindler need money to fund their operations and this quaint little neutral country, known for its banking secrecy, fits that need perfectly. Secrecy and spies go together."

"You still don't know whether that bullet was meant for one of us or not."

"True, but I'm going with the odds it was a sanctioned hit. Professionals only kill when necessary. Somebody wanted that guy dead, not us."

Mack realized Siva wasn't convinced. He changed the subject. "You were about to tell me what Ray said before you agreed to open the account."

"Let's walk and talk," Mack said. He started up the long, gentle hill hoping Siva would follow.

She stayed with him stride for stride.

"Ray said the money in the account was to fund unrest and social disobedience in Russia, aimed directly at the Russian President. It was payback for Russia's attempts to meddle in the US elections, the UK elections, the French elections and the Israeli elections, to name a few. A destabilized Russia would make the Russian President and whoever takes over after him think twice before they try and interfere in other countries affairs again."

Mack took Siva by the elbow and directed her around the corner onto *Rindermarkt*, a narrow, cobblestone pedestrian pathway lined with small shops.

"Who funded the account?" Mack asked.

"The US funded seventy-five percent. Israel provided the rest."

"What about the UK and France?"

"Apparently they didn't have the budget."

Mack grinned. "They're so used to the US funding everything it's become a habit for them."

"We can discuss geopolitics later, okay?"

Mack ignored her sarcasm. "Why did Israel agree to provide some funding?"

"That's the reason Ray wanted me involved. If this operation was successful or even showed promise, the next country targeted is Iran. Israel is more than eager to see the theocracy in Iran fall and fall quickly."

"And your connection to Iran makes you a natural to run that operation."

"That's why I couldn't say no. I still have family in Iran, many of whom are persecuted on a daily basis because my father married a Catholic."

Mack stopped and pointed with his chin at a sandy brown building with a double archway. The sign above read: *Das Alten Buch (The Old Book)*.

"This is where we're going. Before we go in, you need to know a few things." Mack peeked in the window then took a step back. "Peter is American but living off the grid. He has a Swiss passport but it's a forgery and Peter is not his real name."

"Why is he off the grid?"

"He used to work for Ray Gunn in Ray's previous life. He was Ray's most effective agent, if you know what I mean, and made more than his share of enemies, many of who still want him dead and even more who would willingly sell him out to make that happen."

"Then why does he own an antique book store open to the public?"

"He doesn't work the store. He stays in the back repairing old books while his daughter runs the store."

Siva looked at Mack and furrowed her brow. "How do you know all this?"

"You know how I believe Ray has a sixth sense?"

Siva nodded.

"Before I left for Zürich, Ray and I met for a beer in Ray's favorite bar in Chicago, that little Czech dive bar he frequents near Logan Square. During our second beer, he gave me Peter's name and location in case we ran into a problem. I'd say we have a problem."

Mack pushed through the door and stepped inside the bookstore followed closely by Siva.

A trim blonde Mack took to be around twenty years old gave him the once-over like she didn't want him in her store. She made her way over to Siva and said, "We close in five minutes."

$

# CHAPTER 5

Mack ignored the young blonde's disapproving glare and peered around the bookshelves searching for a small camera. As he scanned the room, he felt the blonde scrutinizing him with a doubtful eye. It was a silent inquisition.

She carried an air of detachment. It told Mack she'd do what's necessary to defend what's hers. Mack shot a quick glance over to her and realized she was sizing him up and anticipating her countermeasures.

Mack brought his mind back to the task at hand.

Gunn said the camera allowed Peter to see who was in the shop. The miniature camera was located somewhere with a full view of the store. He was to look directly into the camera and give the signal.

Mack located the camera, inconspicuous between a set of old bibles. He coughed into his right hand then patted his chest twice with his left hand.

The phone behind the counter rang. The young blonde strolled over and picked up the phone. She silently nodded three times then returned the phone to its cradle. She looked at Mack and tilted her head toward the door behind the counter.

Mack nodded thanks as he walked by. He turned the door handle, cautiously pushed the door open and stepped inside. Siva was close behind.

The room was cool, dry and immaculate. Bookshelves filled with leather-bound books lined three walls. Mack sniffed in the strong smell. The room smelled like old leather with a hint of wet wool.

Sitting behind a large wooden desk was a slender man with long gray hair down to his shoulders and a long gray beard. An old book was open on the desk in front of him. Pulled down low over the book was a large round magnifying glass on the end of a retractable swinging arm. Wrapped around the thick magnifying glass was a muted fluorescent light.

Directly behind the desk was a tall bookshelf filled with newly-repaired leather bound books.

Siva closed the door behind her and turned the deadbolt lock.

Mack noticed the man's hands were hidden under the desk. "Our mutual friend strongly suggested I make your acquaintance, Peter," Mack said and raised his hands to indicate he wasn't armed. "I was told you were the best antique book restorer in Zürich." That was the phrase he was instructed to give.

A slight smile graced Peter's lips. He rose from his chair and came around the desk. Peter was a few inches taller than Mack but weighed a good twenty pounds less. "How is the old son of a gun?" he asked.

Hearing the requisite phrase, Mack said, "The old son of a gun is as cranky as ever and he sends his regards."

The smile disappeared from Peter's lips. "If you're here, it means you have a problem and need my help."

Mack held out his hand. "My names Billy and this is Siva."

Peter squeezed Mack's hand then smiled at Siva.

Mack said, "We have a problem but we don't exactly know to what extent."

Mack's phone rang and he fished it out of his pocket.

"Speak of the devil, it's Ray Gunn." He put the phone on speaker and held it in front of him.

"Hi Ray, I'm with Siva and Peter."

"Billy, Siva..." There was a short pause before Gunn said, "Peter, it's been awhile."

"Still not used to calling me Peter, are you Ray?"

"I don't know if I will ever get used to that."

"Don't worry about it, my earthly existence only depends on it," Peter said, only half joking.

"Thank you for this Peter," Gunn said. "First off, this line is secure so we can talk freely. Billy, fill us in on what's happened."

Mack explained about the missing money at Keller Bank, the man who followed Siva and him to the café and then to the Brasserie before he was killed. He gestured for Siva to add anything he omitted. She shook her head no.

"Inside the Brasserie next to the Opera House, the man approached us, pulled out a gun and escorted us out. On the top step, someone put a large hole in his head. We have no idea where the shot came from. That's when we came here. We didn't see the shoot-"

Peter held up his hand and interrupted Mack. "Are you directly involved in this Ray?"

"Indirectly," Gunn said. "A former colleague asked for a recommendation and I suggested Siva be the account holder."

"At which alphabet does the former colleague work?" Peter asked.

"He was a NOC (*pronounced knock*) for the Company working closely with our sister organization in Jerusalem. He ran both Kosovo operations for the Company."

"What's a NOC?" Mack asked.

"It stands for non-official cover. NOCs are agents who don't officially work for the CIA. Official agents have diplomatic cover and, if caught, are sent home. NOCs don't have that cover. If a NOC is caught they usually rot in jail, or worse."

"Why then would anyone want to be a NOC?" Mack asked.

"Money," Gunn answered. "A NOC has access to funds that aren't closely monitored. The bosses at Langley turn a blind eye to the transactions in those accounts, as long as the NOC doesn't get too greedy."

"Do you think this NOC took the money?" Siva asked.

Peter snorted then said, "That joker isn't smart enough to do that. I'm frankly surprised that idiot is still alive?" Peter rolled his eyes. "He always was a lucky bastard. I can't believe he's still working with the Company."

"He's freelance now. He's been living in Liechtenstein for the past ten years."

"Counting the money he has stashed there."

"That's why the Company chose him for this operation. He knows how to move money without leaving a trail. He only needed a proxy. That's where Siva came in. She did something like this a few years ago so she knew how it worked."

Peter sat on the corner of his desk. He rubbed his thumbnail against his teeth as the thought.

"Based on my experience, whoever steals intel money knows what they're doing. The most likely options are someone on the inside at the CIA or Mossad or our freelance buddy padding his retirement fund. My second guess is someone inside the bank. I had a third option but since she is standing in front of me, I guess I can rule her out."

Peter looked at Siva to see her reaction.

Siva didn't move, didn't twitch. A few seconds passed before a 'fuck you' smirk grew on her olive-skinned face.

Peter lifted his right hand. "Sorry, had to be sure."

"You can eliminate the freelancer," Gunn said. "The Company has been sitting on him from the start."

"Since we're talking about Keller Bank my gut tells me someone inside one of the two agencies is working with someone inside the bank."

"What about a hacker?" Mack asked. "The Russians, the Chinese, the North Koreans all have sophisticated hacking operations."

"Only if you're talking about targeting some mom and pop operation with limited security or some idiot dumb enough to give out his log-in info," Peter replied.

"They're getting better but still don't have the skills to get past Keller's firewalls," Gunn added.

Peter pushed himself up from his desk. "As I see it you have two problems. The first problem is to find the money and get it back while avoiding the people who want to keep you from doing just that.

Your life means nothing to them. The second problem is you never find the money and somehow survive. You'll have a target on your back for the rest of your life. Both agencies will assume you stole the money and will hunt you down." Peter looked at Mack with resolve. "If this happens, nobody, not even the legendary Ray Gunn, can protect you. If the Mossad wants to find you, they find you. The only good news is you won't see the bullet coming and your death will be instantaneous."

"That's comforting," Mack said. "That means we can't just sit and wait to get shot."

"What options do we have?" Siva asked.

Peter walked back around his desk, closed the old book lying on top of his desk and pushed the magnifying glass aside. He reached under his desk and pulled out a silver pistol with wooden grips. He handed it to Mack.

"This is a .45 caliber Colt. It will stop anything short of a charging Moose. Just aim and fire. There are seven rounds in the magazine." He handed Mack a second magazine. "If you need more than two magazines, say your prayers and make things right with your maker."

Mack placed his phone on the desk, studied the Colt then gripped it to get a feel.

"That's the only option you can come up with?"

Siva asked, not hiding her frustration.

"What are you carrying?" Peter asked.

Siva blushed as she reached into her handbag and pulled out a black Glock 10, automatic.

Peter whistled then said, "You can handle the kick from that mother?"

"Why? Because I'm a woman?"

"No, I'd say the same thing to Rambo if he pulled out that piece."

Gunn's voice bellowed through the speaker on Mack's phone, "Don't worry about Siva. She can handle any piece you give her."

"Sorry I doubted you," Peter said.

Siva's 'fuck you' smirk returned.

"Let's go over the options," Gunn said.

Peter leaned back in his leather chair and went back to rubbing his thumbnail across his teeth. A few seconds later, he sat forward and said, "Based on what little we know, my experience tells me Siva and Billy will do better if they split up. Siva, you're likely the one they want. Billy, at this point, your collateral damage. If we use that to our advantage, you can be more effective being apart from Siva."

Mack said, "I don't like Siva being on her own. Until we figure out who took the money, I'm staying with her."

"Billy," Gunn said, his voice tinny through the phone. "Listen to Peter. He's still breathing because he's the best at assessing life and death situations and the risks involved. That being said, I have someone in Zürich who will shadow Siva. She'll get the protection she needs."

$

# CHAPTER 6

Beat Keller stepped out from under the *Relaxation Grotto's* waterfall shower and stood in front of the hot air blowers, turning slowly to dry off. After drying off, he wrapped the towel around his waist and faced Mercy Geissel.

"I mulled over our predicament." Keller opened his towel flashing Geissel then re-wrapped it tighter around his waist. "I'm giving Khandelwal and his team one day to find out who stole the money and get it back in the account. If they fail, you bring in Bella. If we go with her, I expect to her to have the missing money back in less than twenty-four hours. I don't care how."

"I will be on top of this until the money is returned. We will get the money back," Geissel said with absolute certainty. "I promise."

"You better be right Mercy. More than you care to know depends on it."

Geissel turned to leave.

"Tell Khandelwal to be in my office in ten minutes."

"I'll have him in your office in five minutes. I will fully inform him of our situation and stress how important it is to get this fixed now."

Keller strolled to the corner of the room. A concealed door slid open leading to a private elevator between the *Relaxation Grotto* and Keller's office one floor above. Keller stepped inside, turned and glared at Geissel. His daily meditation was disturbed and he blamed Mercy Geissel.

As soon as the elevator doors closed, Geissel spun around and ran across the tile floor. She flung open the door and broke into a sprint. She had to get to Khandelwal in case Keller called him.

She raced up the steps and ran down the hall, her heels clacking rhythmically as she ran. In front of

Khandelwal's office she caught her breath, straightened her hair then her blouse. She stuck a smile on her face and knocked firmly on his door.

There was no answer. She waited a few seconds then knocked harder. Still no answer. She peered up and down the hall then cautiously pushed open the door and stuck her head in.

The office was vacant but Khandelwal's computer was on. The screen saver had a picture of his three kids: two teenage girls and a young boy.

Geissel stepped inside and slowly closed the door with two hands. Khandelwal's office had a sleek steel desk with a large computer screen on the left side and two closed laptops next to his phone. Papers were strewn across the top of his desk. In the corner, a small sofa and two chairs stood below the double-paned window.

She strolled over to Khandelwal's desk and studied the papers on top of the desk. Over her career, Geissel had perfected the art of reading upside down.

Her eyes quickly went to the account summary for Siva Afari. The account balance read $0.00. Somehow, Khandelwal knew about the missing money. She struggled to read the handwritten notes by Khandelwal. His handwriting was like chicken scratch, nearly illegible.

Geissel leaned down to decipher what Khandelwal had written. She heard the door handle click. She jerked her head up and turned around. She composed herself and kept from blushing — another art she perfected.

Khandelwal stood in the doorway with his hands on his hips. "Can I help you?" He said with a slight Indian accent.

Geissel smiled demurely. "I was looking for a piece of paper so I could leave you a note."

Khandelwal was average height with wide shoulders and a full head of black hair. He marched around his desk, swept his papers into a pile and placed them aside. "Now that I'm here, you don't need to leave a note," Khandelwal said in an accusatory tone.

Geissel caught herself before grimacing and striking a somber pose. "I'm under stress trying to locate missing money from one of our accounts and wasn't thinking."

"I assume you mean the Afari, Double D account?"

Geissel grimaced. "Yes, how did you know?"

"Every time an account has a zero balance, I'm notified." Khandelwal looked at his watch and said, "The boss just texted me and wants me in his office to discuss a problem with an account. Can I assume it's about the Afari account? Tell me what you know."

"It's most likely the Afari account. I don't know much but will fill you in on what I know on our way to Beat's office."

Khandelwal reached over, took the stack of papers from his desktop and placed them inside a plastic folder. "The boss told me to come alone."

Geissel laughed easily. "That's because he wants to keep a lid on this. The fewer people involved the better. You know how people talk."

"I'm just repeating his text," Khandelwal said and headed to the door, his plastic folder under his arm. At the door, he swept his hand toward the hall, gesturing for Geissel to get out of his office.

Geissel smiled easily as she walked by. She wasn't sure how it came across to Khandelwal. In the hall, she waited then walked next to him as they strolled down the hall to Keller's corner office.

She said, "Afari met a man as soon as she left the building. He kept out of sight of our security cameras but we've identified him as William McMillan. Everyone calls him Billy Mack. We found some old press on him. He's former baseball player who now works for BIG Investments, a large, powerful private equity investor in Chicago. He doesn't have an official title and flies under the radar. From what I can tell, he fixes problems."

"What does that mean?" Khandelwal asked.

"One of the name partners of BIG is Ray Gunn, a former high ranking intelligence officer but it doesn't end there. Gunn once ran top secret black ops for an American government agency which we haven't yet identified."

"Let me ask you again," Khandelwal said. "What does that mean?"

"I know you tech guys are not good at math so I'll explain. Two plus two equals black ops spy. Billy Mack is an operative, a black ops spy. BIG is a front for operations and for operatives that take care of problems. In other words, Mack's a bad hombre. He plays by his own rules, if you know what I mean."


Keller's office door was open and he was standing next to his desk quietly talking with his assistant, Liv. When he finished, Liv took a file off Keller's desk and walked briskly out of the office. She didn't acknowledge Khandelwal or Geissel as she strolled out.

Keller said, "Take a seat Lee."

He glared at Geissel. "Mercy will you please

close the door on your way out?"

Geissel hastily replied, "It would be better for Lee if I sat in." She sat in the chair next to Khandelwal and arched her back to indicate she was eager to begin.

Keller looked over at Khandelwal.

Khandelwal easily shook his head then shrugged his shoulders as if he had no idea what she talking about.

"Mercy," Keller said, "this is technology meeting. When we get to the Afari account, I'll have Liv come and get you. You can also bring me the Afari and Mack files I asked for."

Geissel slumped back in her chair then sat up and arched her back again like she just had a thought. "Why don't the three of us compare notes on the missing money then I can leave you two alone while I go and make some phone calls to solve our problem?"

Keller pointed to the door. "Liv will come get you when you're needed."

Keller and Khandelwal watched Geissel leave and reluctantly meander down the hall. By the way she walked it was obvious she was trying to figure out a reason to come back and join the meeting.

Keller walked over to the door, closed it and turned the lock. Walking back to his desk, he said, "In the few minutes you've had to look into this, what can you tell me?"

Khandelwal opened the plastic folder, leafed through the papers and pulled out his notes. "The money was transferred out of the Afari account in two installments. The first was for $40 million to a bank in Austria then sent on to Southern Bank in Miami. The remaining $60 million was wired directly to the same bank in Miami."

"Who approved the transfers? According to Mercy and Marek Gullberg, Afari claims she didn't order any monies transferred or approve any such transfers. She was adamant no one except her knew her approval code."

Khandelwal raised his eyebrows to show his skepticism. "The palm reader and key code to the client rooms show Afari was in the bank at the time of the transfer, her account number was properly inputted and her personal approval code was used. The proper protocols were followed so there is no reason to believe Afari did not initiate the transfer. On the off chance she didn't, whoever initiated the wire transfer was able to erase the URL and any trace of their involvement. Since this is a Double D account, I recommend we bring Afari back in, grill her and see what she has to say."

"Easier said than done. When she stormed out of here earlier today, she made her intentions clear. Plus, we have an idea of the intel agencies behind this account but don't know who inside the agencies funded the account. I learned early on not to dig too deep where intel accounts are concerned."

Khandelwal said, "It feels to me that Afari is in bed with someone nefarious, someone likely inside one of the two agencies. According to Mercy, Afari met someone in front of the bank. He goes by the name Billy Mack and he was shrewd enough to stay out of view of our security cameras. She's convinced he's an operative who works in the shadows. Did Mercy give you any information on Afari and Mack?"

Keller shook is head and frowned. "I'm waiting on the files. Mercy's convinced Mack is involved. If this Billy Mack is a serious player and her theory is true, it confirms Afari's involved, wittingly or not. Let's play this out. What else you have?"

Khandelwal pulled the papers from his folder and scanned them. "I had a very short conversation with the president of Southern Bank in Miami but he was close-lipped. He made it clear that if he gave us any information without his client's approval he would be sued, or worse. He sounded worried on the phone. The only way we'll find out anything from Southern bank is if we bring in lawyers or law enforcement and get a subpoena. By that time, the money and any evidence will be long gone and we'll be at a dead end."

"Have you run background checks on all employees?" Keller asked.

"That is never done unless you personally order it."

"I did."

"I never got the order."

"Shit. Do it as soon as we're done here. What other options do we have?"

"We hire Dmitri Askov to hack into Southern Bank. If he can't get into the bank's system, no one can."

Keller exhaled loudly as he drummed his fingers on his desk. "I hate using hackers. Each time we use them they learn more about our system and pretty soon we're their next target."

Khandelwal waited patiently while Keller mulled his decision.

Keller finally said, "Do it. The longer we wait the less our chance of success."

Khandelwal shoved his papers back into his folder. "I figured you'd say that. Dmitri is already on it."

Keller glanced at his watch. "He has twenty-four hours. If he fails, we bring in Bella to clean this thing up."

Khandelwal closed his eyes and dropped his chin. "Do you think that's wise? It's dangerous to our reputation and *she's* dangerous."

"If it were only a million bucks," Keller replied, "I'd replace it myself but this is a hundred million and a Double D account. If Dmitri fails, I can't afford not to bring Bella in."

Khandelwal prayed Dmitri would find the money and steal it back. If Dmitri failed, he'd be forced to work with Bella and, to make matters worse, it would be on her terms. He had to buy time for Dmitri. "I strongly recommend we find this Billy Mack, flex our muscles with a come to Jesus meeting. The evidence tells me he and Afari are involved. If he is an operative, he's probably Afari's handler. He's either her co-conspirator, or worse, he used her to steal the money."

Down the hall, in the doorway of her corner office, Geissel turned and peeked back at Keller's office before silently closing her office door.

She hesitated before marching over to her

briefcase resting against the wall underneath the window. She glanced back at the door then squatted and removed an untraceable flip phone. She stared down at the number pad deciding whether to make the call or let things play out. It would be better if she knew what Keller and Khandelwal were saying and what they've learned so far.

She turned on the flip phone and punched in the phone number. The phone on her desk rang before she pushed the send button.

Her assistant Maddie was calling her. She closed her flip phone and stuck it in her pocket.

She lifted the receiver from its cradle. "Yes?"

"Ms. Geissel, I have a Mickey Guiliani and an Israel Joe Paletz on the phone for you."

"Take a message."

"Ummm, you want to take this," Maddie said with a twinge of fear in her voice.

"Did they say who they were with?" Geissel asked knowing the answer.

"Just a sec." There was a moment of silence. "It's regarding the Afari account. Is there a problem I should know about?"

"No, no, they're with the company that helped set up the account. Tell them I'm finishing up a call and will be with them in a minute."

Geissel hung up the phone and sat back. Her leather desk chair squeaked loudly, startling her. She realized she was on edge and took a number of deep breaths to calm herself. She braced herself then hesitantly reached for the phone. Dealing with pissed-off intelligence agents rarely ended well.

$

# CHAPTER 7

Mack leaned his hip against Peter's desk and studied the Colt .45 Peter had given him. He slid it into his waistband and dropped the extra magazine into his coat pocket. "When is Siva's shadow expected?" he asked.

"Just a sec," Gunn said.

Hushed voices came through the phone followed by a period of silence.

While waiting for Gunn to come back on the phone, Mack mulled over how to convince Gunn he wasn't leaving Siva's side. He had to be careful with his words. Confronting Gunn in front of Peter was a career-threatening move.

Gunn came back to the phone. "He's at Zürich's main train station waiting for my call. He has a car waiting and I only need to give him the destination address."

"You understand, Ray, he can't come here... for obvious reasons," Peter said.

"That would make things easier, Peter."

"If it were only me, I'd accommodate you but my daughter works out front. She can take care of herself but she's exposed out there in the shop and I won't risk revealing my location."

"Understood. Can you recommend a safe place where there's little risk of Siva being seen? Someplace where you'd be comfortable going."

"There is no place I'm comfortable going. I burned all my bridges so making contact with anyone from my old days is *verboten*. Everyone from my past thinks I'm dead and many are still celebrating." Peter stretched his arms over his head and yawned. "Where's the shadow staying?"

"In *Niederdorf*, at a hotel on *Zähringerstrasse*, near the public library."

"That's close to an apartment I keep," Peter said

then noticed the confusion on Mack's face. "Just in case."

Mack thought about the world Peter lived in and nodded like he understood why he 'kept an apartment... just in case.'

"I'll have my daughter take Siva to the Safari Bar down the street from the apartment and wait with her until the shadow arrives."

"The Safari Bar? Your old hangout?" Gunn replied. "Do you think that's wise?"

"Hilda will be there and knows the bar. That makes it as safe as any place in town."

"I'm going with them," Mack said.

Peter snorted out a laugh. "No, you're not."

"Give me one good reason why I shouldn't"

"Billy, I'll let you in on a little secret. My daughter has been through hell and back. As a result, she is prepared for anything that comes her way. She is more dangerous than you, Siva and me combined." Peter saw the doubt in Mack's eyes. "Given our precarious situation, she's been trained in the necessary arts. She will put a hurt on anyone threatening her and walk away without a scratch or even leaving a trace. Trust me when I say, I've put my life in her hands more than once."

"That little girl out front?" Mack said skeptically, pointing at the door. "You gotta be kidding me."

The sly grin on Peter's face unnerved Mack.

"You know the old saying, 'it's not the size of the dog in the fight,'" Peter said.

"It's the size of the fight in the dog," Mack replied. "But I have a hard time-"

"Excuse me," Siva said, interrupting. "I can take care of myself and this is my decision. It's my life on the line and if Peter's daughter is well trained, that works for me. Besides, whoever is after me won't expect me to be with a young woman who can pass as my daughter. It's a good cover."

Siva walked over to the phone lying on the desk and leaned down over the speaker. "Unless you have an objection Ray, she's with me."

"Your call," Gunn replied.

Mack bit his tongue knowing that when Siva made up her mind it was no use arguing.

"Siva, you can't go back to your hotel," Peter said. He reached into his desk drawer, pulled out a set of keys on it and handed them to Siva. "Here are the keys to the apartment. You can use it while we clean up this mess. After you meet up with the shadow, Hilda will bring you there."

Mack asked, "Do I need to arrange for different accommodations?"

Peter stared at the phone anticipating Gunn to say something. After a minute of strained silence, Peter said, "Ray, you want to tell him or should I?"

"It's better coming from you, Peter."

Mack didn't like the way Peter was looking at him and said, "Are you about to tell me I'm on my own?"

"No," Peter said and tried to smile reassuringly. He saw the look in Mack's eyes and knew his smile wasn't working. "You're a decoy."

"Oh great, a sitting duck. Why?"

"Billy," Gunn said, "thinks of this as a sacrifice bunt. When you played baseball and the manager gave you the sacrifice bunt sign, you didn't question the manager, you bunted. This is the same thing albeit with more riding on the outcome. It's the right thing to do."

"As far as I can remember, no one was ever shot while bunting."

"Relax," Peter said. He paused for a few seconds then added, "The only people who know what team you're on are the three of us, Hilda and Siva. As far as whoever made off with the money, they're interested in Siva. They will want to know how you're involved and what you know. Once they determine you don't know anything, you're a loose end. Loose ends don't get cleaned up until after the operation."

"How does that help Siva?"

"There's a much greater possibility the player or players in their search for Siva will expose themselves trying to figure out who you are. In this business, the element of surprise is an important tool. Confusion gives us, gives Siva, better odds. Go about your business as if nothing has happened."

"In other words, I've got nothing to do and all day to do it," Mack said facetiously.

"It's nice to meet a fellow Styx fan," Peter said with a chuckle.

Mack grinned and said, "I always hated being a role player as much as sitting on the bench and that's what you're telling me to do now."

"Billy," Gunn said loudly to get Mack's full attention. "Trust us, we've done this before. You've never worried about your safety before. If that's the case, I can arrange for someone to watch over you."

Mack wasn't about to agree to have a babysitter, especially in front of Siva. "Fine, I'm the decoy." Mack patted the Colt .45 in his waistband. "What are the risks a decoy faces?"

"They won't shoot you," Peter said with a smirk. "They may grab you, torture you until you tell them what they want to hear. When they are finished with you, they'll wrap a heavy chain around your feet and drop in the deepest part of Lake Zürich. Between two and three hundred feet down the pressure will crush your insides, killing you instantly. You won't feel-"

"Stop it," Gunn said cutting off Peter, "odds are no one is going to do anything to you, Billy except figure out who you are and how you're involved. Most likely someone will approach you and try to trick you into divulging information so they can learn more about you and Siva."

"So I wander the streets of Zürich waiting for some spook to approach me then torture me before killing me?" Mack said, half joking, half mocking.

"Only if you look guilty," Peter said with a laugh. He added, "Billy, very few people know you're in Zürich. Act like a tourist taking in this old city."

"We use your anonymity to our advantage. There is one caveat though." Gunn paused, unnerving Mack. "The Intel community is not a world you understand. That means you have to decide how far you want to get involved, and more importantly, if you can handle whatever you take on."

Mack looked at Siva and had his answer. "I gotta do what I gotta do."

"Billy, you're entering a world where the guilty look innocent and the innocent are made to look guilty, by design." Gunn said.

"If that's the case, what do I need to know?"

"Watch your six and trust your gut."

"That's easier said than done."

"Yes it is."

"Does that approach apply to Keller and his bank?"

With no hesitation Gunn said, "Yes and no. Beat Keller is typical Swiss and keeps his cards close to his chest. Given where the money came from, he's probably shitting bricks right about now... if he's innocent. He knows the repercussions of losing intel money. If he knows some of the money is from Mossad, guilty or innocent, he's already wet himself and will likely expose his hand to get the money back. Using that as our starting point, I'll contact Keller and arrange a meeting with you as Siva's representative. Keller will assume you're with one of the intel agencies and go into hyper drive trying to figure out which one. He will also alert his security team. They'll try and throw a ring around you and figure out what makes you tick. That's what I'd do."

"Keller has unlimited resources," Peter added, "and he'll use every one of them if he has to."

"Peter, you knew Keller better than I ever did," Gunn said. "The three of us should come up with a plan for Billy's meeting."

Peter said, "You can bet your last dollar Keller will not agree to meet at the bank. He'll choose a place that gives him an advantage as well as increased security."

Peter reached across the desk and punched a button on his desk phone. Without looking up, he said, "Siva can you please unlock the door?"

As soon as Siva unlocked the door, the handle turned and the door slowly swung open. The young blonde took one step into the office.

"Hilda, this is Siva. Can you please take her to the Safari Bar? She is meeting someone there. Once he arrives, take them to the apartment in *Niederdorf*. When you get there, give her one of our phones and show her how to use it. Then wait there until you hear from me."

"Right now?" Hilda asked.

Peter nodded. "Please."

Hilda turned to face Siva and held out her hand. "Give me your phone."

"Why? My phone is untraceable," Siva said.

Hilda wiggled her fingers gesturing for Siva to hand over her phone.

Siva reached into her handbag, pulled out her phone and reluctantly dropped it in Hilda's hand.

Hilda powered down the phone, popped open the back and removed the battery. She handed the phone back to Siva. "I'll give the battery back in when this is over."

Hilda strolled out of the office.

Mack walked over to Siva. "Be careful."

"You too Billy," she said and kissed him firmly. She turned and followed Hilda out into the bookstore.

Mack closed the door behind Siva and locked the deadbolt. "What can I expect?"

"Watch your back... and your front," Gunn said.

Mack tried to read Peter's expression. Nothing. He asked, "What's the first step?"

"I call Keller and arrange the meeting. Sit tight." Gunn said then hung up without waiting for a reply.

$

Thirty minutes later, Gunn called back on Peter's private line. Peter punched the speaker button on the desk phone. "Is the meeting arranged?"

"Done, the meeting is at ten o'clock tonight in the town of Zollikon." Gunn read off the address.

"That's Keller's house on Lake Zürich, just outside the city limits," Peter said.

"I don't like this," Mack said. "Why can't we meet in a public place, a busy restaurant or hotel lobby?"

Gunn said, "Keller was nervous but trying to hide it. His voice was weak and he over-explained himself. He bucked up at the end. That was when he was adamant the meeting be held at his ultra-secure private residence."

"I've been inside Keller's house," Peter said. "It's a fortress with impenetrable walls on three sides."

"Why only three sides?" Mack asked.

"It's on Lake Zürich and the shoreline has an electronic barrier impossible to breach without alarms going off. He wasn't about to block one of the best lake views money can buy with a physical wall."

"I still don't like it," Mack said, gasping as if he had no choice but to give in. "What do we want to accomplish at this meeting?"

Gunn said, "By the questions he asked me, he's convinced you're with the CIA. I didn't dispel him of that notion. If he asks directly, deflect. That will convince him."

"Don't deflect, deny," Peter said. "Operatives are expected to lie and Keller knows that."

"Good point," Gunn said. "Convince him you're there to help him get the money back and smooth things over with the agencies. Don't volunteer any information but act like you have his best interests at heart. He'll be skeptical and we can use that to our advantage."

Peter nodded in agreement and said, "Try to get him to walk you through what happened and what he's doing inside the bank to recover the money. Demand he give you the names and responsibilities of all Keller employees. Be insistent but don't overplay your hand."

"And demand access to his system," Gunn added. "He won't give it to you but that will put him on the defensive. Then start asking questions about who had access to Siva's account within the bank and demand to speak with each of them. If he resists, threaten him by using thinly-veiled implications, like *'my superiors don't appreciate their money being stolen, if you know what I mean.'*"

"Only threaten him as a last resort," Peter said. "The important thing is to get as much information as you can out of him. If he's not involved then he knows he's in big trouble so he'll reveal more information than Swiss bankers legally can."

"Billy, you've done this routine many times in your job. It's just like digging into a troubled investment or a company going down the tubes. Approach it like that. Ask questions, listen to his answers and his tone of voice. Listen carefully because the key will be what he's not saying."

Mack looked at his watch. "The meeting is in an hour. I need directions and transportation."

"I've arranged for a man to prep you before going in. He knows Keller and can give you guidance. While your inside, he'll wait nearby and give you a ride back to town."

"Who is this guy?"

"You've already met him, so to speak. He'll be waiting for you at the *Tiefenbrunnen* train station."

$

# CHAPTER 8

Before leaving the bookstore, Hilda stopped at the front counter, tapped on the computer keyboard and studied the screen. She turned the screen for Siva to see. On the screen was a live view of the street outside. "Do you recognize anyone from earlier today? Look at clothes, hair for anything distinctive, anything that jogs your memory."

Siva examined the screen looking at each person on the street then checked the windows in every building lining the street. "No," she finally answered, "but, that doesn't mean anything."

Hilda turned the screen back and gave the street a second scan. Satisfied, she said, "Time to go. Keep a sharp eye out. If anything bothers you, tell me but do so as if we're having a casual conversation."

"Of course," Siva answered as she followed Hilda to the front door. Before stepping out, Siva slipped on a pair of dark sunglasses, covering a large part of her face.

Hilda locked the front door to the bookstore and said, "We'll take a roundabout way to our rendezvous. Stay close to me but act like you're leading the way."

Hilda slipped her hand inside Siva's elbow. "Go up and take the first left," she said in a low voice. "We stay on the pedestrian streets until we get near the Safari Bar. Follow my instructions and we'll get there safely."

They strolled down the narrow cobblestone streets acting like they were out window-shopping. Every second block, they stopped in front of a shop and peered in the display window. Each time they stopped, Hilda pointed at an item in the window and said something. Siva smiled and nodded as if she agreed. All the while, they were both studying their surroundings through the reflections in the windows.

At a busy intersection, Hilda said, "We go left here and down the hill. At the first street, turn right.

These last two roads are always bustling. Move at a hurried but measured pace and keep a sharp eye out for anyone covertly eyeing us."

They turned onto *Zähringerstrasse*, a one-way street with the traffic coming at them. Parked cars lined both sides of the road, occupying every parking space. Hilda kept a brisk pace, as if they were running late.

Across the street from the Safari Bar, Hilda squeezed Siva's elbow to get her to stop.

"We're being followed," Hilda whispered.

"The man in the black sport coat?" Siva asked.

Hilda glanced at a storefront down the street. She saw a man with a long blonde ponytail pulled tight, wearing the black leather sport coat, dark pants and black boots. He turned and looked in the other direction.

"That's him. He's been following us for two blocks. Either he's an amateur or he wants us to see him."

When there was a break in the traffic, Hilda said, "We go straight inside the bar. Once inside, I'll canvass the room for the man Mr. Gunn arranged for us to meet."

"How do you know what he looks like?"

"He'll make a subtle gesture."

"I get the feeling you've done this before."

Hilda grinned but didn't answer.

Inside the Safari Bar, Hilda and Siva peered around the dark interior. The bar stood in the center of the room surrounded on all four sides by orange and black striped stools. The bartender acknowledged them with a nod. Sitting at the bar facing the door was an old man nursing a glass of beer with an unlit cigarette between his fingers. He smiled at Siva. Both front teeth were missing.

Hilda pointed to a table against the back wall. The table stood beneath a "WC" sign pointing to the left, to a back hallway leading to the bathrooms. "Over there," she said. She marched over to the table and sat with her back against the wall.

Siva hesitated.

"Sit next to me," Hilda said, not taking her eyes off the entrance.

Siva turned, sat and nearly jumped out of her seat, startled by the bartender, with a bar towel slung over his shoulder, standing next to their small round table.

"What can I get you ladies?" he asked in flawless American English.

Siva composed herself. "Black tea with lemon," she said as she removed her sunglasses.

"Southern Comfort with one ice cube," Hilda said.

"How old are you?" The bartender asked with skeptical look in his eye.

"Twenty."

"If you want alcohol its beer or wine only."

Hilda gave him a look telling him she didn't approve.

The bartender simply grinned.

"I'll have a mineral water then."

As the bartender meandered away, Hilda dug through her handbag and pulled out her phone. She showed the phone to Siva and said, "Keep watch on the front door while I make this call."

Hilda punched the number in her phone then looked up. Standing in the entrance to the back hallway, a foot to the right of their table was the man with the tight blonde ponytail. His hands were stuffed in the pockets of his black leather sport coat.

Hilda slowly lowered her phone and her other hand down to her lap, underneath the table.

"Put hands on table, both you," the man said with a heavy Russian accent.

Siva placed her hands flat on the table.

Hilda didn't move.

"You are too much beautiful to shoot. Put hands on table."

Hilda put her hands on the table and held them like she was praying.

A big smile broke out on the man's face. "Beautiful and sly like fox. Now, put mobile phone on table."

Hilda sniffed showing her contempt then reached down and placed the phone on the table.

The man kept his eyes glued to Hilda and pointed at Siva. "You are Siva Afari, no?"

"Yes," Siva replied.

"Who are you?" he said to Hilda and smiled to show her he already knew her name.

"That depends," Hilda answered. "If you're here to hurt my friend or me, I'm your worst nightmare. Who are you?"

The man reached down and grabbed Hilda's phone off the table and took a selfie. He then tapped in a number and sent the selfie in text message. He handed the phone to Hilda.

"Answer phone when it ring."

Siva shifted in her chair in case she needed to make a run for it.

"Stay in chair," the man said then smiled like he would hurt Siva if she moved.

Hilda's phone rang, startling her.

"Put on speaker," the man ordered.

Hilda tapped the speaker button and held the phone out in front of her.

"This is Ray Gunn," said the voice coming from the phone.

Siva snatched the phone from Hilda, turned off the speaker and stuck the phone in her ear.

"Ray? Is this the man you arranged as protection?"

Siva tapped the speaker button and lowered the phone's volume.

"Yes, the man with you is Vlad. He's agreed to help. Not that you and Hilda need help but given what little we know, reinforcements are always good and Vlad is the best in the business at protection, among other things."

Vlad puffed out his chest and smiled broadly.

"You three need to go to the pre-arranged spot and wait for further instructions," Gunn said. The phone line went dead and began beeping.

The bartender arrived with Siva's tea and Hilda's mineral water. He placed them on the table then turned and faced Vlad. "What can I get you?"

"Bottle vodka to go, please."

"No can do. You gotta drink it here."

Vlad dug into his pocket and pulled out a one hundred Swiss franc note and waved it in front of the bartender's face. "Maybe this change mind."

"Sorry, we don't carry cheap Russian vodka."

Vlad took out a five hundred franc note. "You have vodka from Sweden?"

The bartender reached over and gingerly took the money from Vlad's hand. "A bottle of Purity coming up," he said as he walked away.

Siva stood. "I don't think it's wise for you to bring a bottle of vodka with."

"It is for when job is over. Is Russian tradition to celebrate victory with vodka."

Vlad held out his hand to help Hilda rise from her chair.

She slapped his hand away.

"I think maybe you are what you say... *nightmare*. Mr. Gunn say to me you very tough, very smart. I like you before I meet you."

A thin smile creased Hilda's lips.

"How we do this?" Vlad asked.

"Siva and I walk together," Hilda replied. "You stay close behind. The apartment is only two blocks from here so it won't take but a couple minutes."

Waiting for the bartender to bring the bottle of vodka, Vlad said, "You are called Hilda, yes?"

Hilda nodded.

"You much beautiful and Mr. Gunn say you very tough and I not to be fooled of you size. How you do it?"

"Motivation," Hilda said.

"I hope to see this motivation."

"I hope you don't because that means we've run into trouble."

"When this over, you come to Moscow and teach me what you know."

The bartender walked out from the back and handed a long, clear bottle to Vlad. "Enjoy, comrade."

"Let's go," Siva said nervously. "You two can finish your... whatever this is, once we're safely inside the apartment."

$

# CHAPTER 9

Mercy Geissel sat at her desk and gazed at the phone knowing she had to sound confident and convince the two men on the other end of the line she had everything under control. They were professionals and could smell weakness and fear even through the phone.

"Mr. Giuliani, Mr. Paletz, what can I do for you?"

"We have a problem with the Afari account."

Geissel needed to buy some time. "Can you please identify yourself so I know with whom I'm speaking?"

"This is Mickey Giuliani." His voice was raspy from years of cigar smoking. "When will Ms. Afari's money be back in her account?"

The tone of his voice irritated Geissel. She quickly composed herself. "That is a question for Siva Afari. Our records show Ms. Afari initiated the wire transfer. I can send you corroborating evidence. She was here at the time of the wire transfer and she went through the proper protocol."

"This is Israel Joe Paletz speaking. We know that's not the case."

Geissel thought for a second. Guiliani had an American accent so he was CIA and Paletz had a Yiddish accent so he was Mossad. It was time for her to play their game. "If you have evidence showing otherwise, please share it with me so I can help you."

"That's not how this works," Giuliani said. "You will provide us with your internal records pertaining to the Afari account, including who in Keller Bank had access to the account. It's easier if you just give us unfettered access to your system."

As soon as Giuliani finished, Paletz added, "We also want your records provided to FINMA *(Swiss Financial Market Supervisory Authority)*, your internal security records and the names of the employees in your Security, Compliance and IT departments."

"Gentlemen, you know that's not going to happen."

"Mercy," Giuliani said. "May I call you Mercy?"

"Of course," Geissel answered with a little more of a lilt in her voice than she wanted.

"Thank you... Mercy."

The way Giuliani enunciated *'Mercy'* annoyed Geissel but she kept calm, silent.

"Mercy... we're operating under the presumption this was an inside job. Someone inside your bank decided to fund their retirement account with Ms. Afari's money. When we learn who, their retirement will be short-lived. We assume anyone not fully cooperating with us is involved."

"Well Mickey... if I may call you that. I don't respond to threats." Geissel realized what she said and added, "Even those not directed at me."

Silence permeated the phone line. After a few seconds, Geissel sat forward, arched her back and said, "We at the bank are operating under the presumption this was an inside job as well, but from inside one of the intelligence agencies and the agent controlling Ms. Afari and the money. We know Ms. Afari met with a man immediately after she left the bank. I believe he is her controller. He's either an agent or a retired agent."

"We know who she met after she left your bank. We were about to bring Siva Afari in for questioning when our operative had his head blown off coming out of the Brasserie bar," Giuliani said, paused then asked, "Do you know anything about that?"

Geissel digested what Giuliani said. Realizing her silence might convey guilt, she quickly said, "We understand she met with a man who goes by the name Billy Mack as soon as she left the bank. He's either her controller or her accomplice. What did Afari or Mack have to say about the murder?"

Neither Giuliani nor Paletz answered.

Geissel's confidently said, "We're on the same team here. We both want to find out who stole the money. What did they tell you?"

Giuliani huffed and said, "We're still looking for them."

Geissel knew she now had the advantage. "That tells me Siva Afari and Billy Mack are your prime suspects."

"You didn't answer our question. Do you know anything about the murder of our operative?" Paletz asked.

"Of course not. Why would I?"

"You would if you and Afari were working

together," Paletz said.

"That is utterly absurd and insulting. I'm trying to help and you not only accuse me of being a common criminal but also a murderer."

Giuliani cleared his throat. "We'll be back in touch... Mercy. When we do, we expect you to have tracked down the money and have it back in the Afari account or tell us exactly when the money will be back in the account."

The phone line went dead.


Geissel dropped the phone and sprinted out of her office and down the hall. She slowed as she approached Beat Keller's office door. She knocked and opened the door without waiting for a response.

Keller was placing a pile of folders into his briefcase. "Come in," he said sarcastically.

"I just had an interesting phone call," Geissel said as she approached.

Keller removed his suit coat from the back of his chair and threw it on as he strolled around his desk. He stopped, walked back over and lifted his briefcase off the desk. "I'm leaving for a meeting so whatever you have to tell me has to wait until tomorrow."

"With what's going on, are you're going to a

business meeting?"

"No, I have a meeting with Afari's representative. From what I could gather on the call to arrange the meeting, he's a spook with the CIA."

"The meeting is now?"

"In an hour or so."

"Is it with Mickey Giuliani?"

"No, Billy Mack."

"You know that's the man who met Afari outside the bank. Khandelwal and I believe he's working with Afari and is likely the mastermind."

"If that's true, I'll ask him to return the money."

"Where are you meeting him?" Geissel asked in a demanding tone.

"At my place... if that's any of your business."

"Why at your place?"

"I want to keep this under wraps."

"I'm going with you."

"He only agreed to meet with me. You stay here, do your job and get my money back."

$

Geissel watched Keller's private elevator door close then rushed out of his office and down the hall to Khandelwal's office. She formulated her questions as her heels clicked rhythmically on the tile floor. At Khandelwal's office door she knocked and this time she waited.

Khandelwal's muffled voice came through the door. "Enter."

She walked briskly to Khandelwal's desk, waited for him to look up then said, "Beat has directed me to find the missing Afari money and to enlist your help." Before Khandelwal had a chance to reply, she added, "We only have twenty-four hours to do it before Beat brings in outside help. Here's what I need from you."

"Just a second," Khandelwal said, raising his hand. "I need to send this." He typed briefly on his keyboard, tapped the 'enter' key then looked up and smiled at Geissel. "I'll help where I can."

"I'm very happy to hear that. This is a team effort." Geissel flipped open her notebook and clicked her pen. "Where are you on the employee security checks?"

"Most employees are cleared. Our algorithm has a few more machinations to run. So far, we're looking deeper into one person."

"Who might that be and why are you looking

deeper into him?"

"Him? Do you know something I should know?"

Geissel rolled her eyes. "That's the obvious bet since most people working her are men."

"It's Marek Gullberg. He recently opened an account at Zürich Kantonal Bank and there have been two very large deposits recently."

"Good to know. I never trusted him. Keep me informed of what you learn. I suspect he's working with Afari and Mack and that's why he was escorted from the bank."

"He was escorted out because he took a job with a new competitor."

"That's news to me."

"Really? Didn't you do his exit interview?"

Geissel nodded and lowered her eyes. "He lied to me. That puts him at the top of my list of suspects." She scribbled in her notebook.

Khandelwal crossed his arms, sat back and waited.

"What else to you have for me?" Geissel's voice was strong, demanding.

"Besides Gullberg, the only persons with access

to Afari's account are Keller, his assistant Liv, you and me."

Geissel's eyes widened. "Do you think Beat and Liv are involved in this? Why would they?"

"I'm not casting shadows on anyone, I'm just stating facts."

"What do our system logs tell us? Our logs should give a good indication of who's involved."

"The logs show the money was transferred in two lump sums and properly authorized by the account holder, Siva Afari. One transfer went to an Austrian bank and the other went to a bank in Miami. The money sent to Austria was transferred six hours later to the same Miami bank."

"Who approved the transfers?" Geissel asked.

"That's where I'm stumped. There is no data in the logs authorizing the transfers. Whoever approved the transfers knew their way around our system and erased the data. It will take a little time, but I will recover that data."

"What about Afari and Mack? They're the obvious culprits. Have you found anything on them?"

"As I said, according to the system, Afari authorized the transfers." Khandelwal paused and studied Geissel. "Something doesn't sit right and I'm digging deeper. I have a feeler out with the Austrian bank for their wire transfer to Miami. The account in Miami belongs to an offshore company and I've hit a roadblock with who owns the company. Gullberg handled compliance so he's at the top of my list as far as internal suspects. That and his large deposits at Kantonal Bank."

Geissel said, "Gullberg is not going to cooperate. He was escorted from the building under Keller's orders. Security is already tearing his office apart and going through his computer and his files."

Khandelwal smiled confidently. "I'll call him and commiserate with him, tell him Keller made a mistake and I argued for him to stay and transition properly. I'll throw out a few questions and he may unwittingly fill in missing pieces."

"I'd advise you wait and talk to him after he cools down." Geissel jotted a note in her notebook then closed it and stood to go. "I'll get out of your hair and let you get back to work. Keep me up to speed and I'll do likewise."

"Before you go, Mercy, did you know Sunden Capital transferred out their recently deposited $500 million and closed the account?"

Geissel froze and a blank look washed over her face.

She sat back down and said, "I heard they were considering it but... no, I hadn't heard. I'll look into it and find out why."

"I can tell you why," Khandelwal said. "They moved their account to the new competitor. The same bank Gullberg is going to work for. I find that interesting, don't you."

"That's not a coincidence. The new bank's incorporation filings will tell us more. Let me look into those and circle back with you."

Geissel strolled across the office, stopped in the doorway and turned around. "Our focus should remain on Billy Mack and to a lesser extent on Siva Afari. Every instinct I have tells me Mack's the mastermind. From the moment I saw his picture, I knew he was trouble."

Khandelwal waited for Geissel to leave then picked up his phone and hit a speed dial number. "Dmitri, I hope you have good news for me."

$

# CHAPTER 10

Impatient for Peter's phone conversation with Ray Gunn to end, Mack strolled around Peter's pristine bookstore office perusing the titles of the old leather bound books in need of repair.

Scanning the book titles, Mack stopped and reached up to grab a first edition copy of *Moby Dick*.

"Don't touch anything unless you're wearing gloves," Peter yelled while holding his hand over the receiver.

Mack jerked his arm back down. "Sorry."

Peter hung up and waved for Mack to come over. "Ray just spoke with Siva, Hilda and the shadow. His name is Vlad. They're-"

"Vlad the Impaler?" Mack asked, cutting Peter off.

"He just said Vlad and that you knew him."

"I do but I'm surprised Ray didn't say anything to me."

"Would it have mattered?"

Mack realized it wouldn't have mattered. He'd met Vlad in Barcelona when Vlad worked for J Otis Weil before J Otis tried to kill Vlad to tie up a loose end. Gunn normally didn't stomach anyone associated with J Otis Weil but Vlad had a good streak in him as well as a freshly infused motivation to kill J Otis. Gunn took an instant liking to him.

"Siva and Hilda are in good company," Mack said.

"So is Vlad the Impaler," Peter replied. "They're heading to the apartment now."

Mack pointed to leather chair next to the desk. "Can I sit there?"

Peter rolled his eyes.

Mack sat and crossed his legs.

"Herr Schmidt will meet you at the *Tiefenbrunnen* train station. There's a small restaurant at the station. It's the only restaurant. He will fill you in if there's anything new on the missing money. From the restaurant, you can walk to Keller's house. You can see the roof line out the restaurant windows."

"Won't walking over leave me exposed?"

Peter thought about Mack's question then said, "Only if Keller is involved with the missing money. If he is, he won't do anything until he's had a chance to speak with you and see what you know. That makes the two block walk a calculated risk."

"That's not reassuring."

Peter ignored Mack's comment. "Here's what I know about Keller and Keller Bank. Years ago, I heard from a reliable source the Company had an agent inside Keller Bank. The agent was a high-value asset whose identity was known only by those with special access, beyond top secret. I was never able to confirm who. If it were true, the agent may still be inside the bank. What I do know is Beat Keller thrives on information and is a stickler for security. If intel money is missing, all hands will be on deck at the bank to determine where the money went and how to get it back. I expect that's how he'll deal with you."

"Since I don't know anything about the money,

he may figure I'm not worth keeping around."

"Be vague with your answers and act like you know enough to be dangerous. Remember he thinks you're a spook."

"I hope it works."

"We'll soon find out." Peter stood. "I will take you out through the back and down to the tram stop. The last stop on that line is *Tiefenbrunnen* train station."

Peter lifted his wristwatch to eye level and said, "Time to go." He turned around, slid the bookshelf behind the desk to the side revealing a door matching the wall. To the right of the door was numbered keypad. Peter punched in a six-digit code the door slid open to a narrow, unlit and dusty staircase.

"Watch your step," Peter said.


Out on the street, the vintage lighting in the old neighborhood barely reached into the broad entrances of the medieval buildings.

At the first corner, Peter stopped. "This is as far as I go. Follow this street down to the river and take the blue tram heading toward the lake."

Mack stuck out his hand. "Thank you Peter."

Peter shook his hand and said, "Be sure to buy a tram ticket. If you get caught without a ticket, you'll get jammed up."

Peter turned and trudged back up the hill.

Mack stayed close to the walls as he made his way down the cobblestone lane. The old stones were uneven forcing him to lift his feet higher, slowing his normal gait. The last thing he needed was to stumble and lose his focus.

At the bottom of the hill he followed a narrow passageway to the Limmat River. He looked right to see a tram approaching. He jogged to the station, selected his destination and hastily dropped his money in the ticket machine.

Across the river, the large clock face on the church steeple read nine-fifteen.

The tram rolled to a stop and the doors opened automatically. Mack looked both ways before stepping up and into the tramcar. He strolled down the aisle until he found a pair of unoccupied seats. As the tram eased forward, Mack watched a man sprint down the cobblestone lane waving for the tram driver to stop. As the tram rolled away, the man bent and repeatedly slapped his hands on his thighs. His eyes never left Mack.

Mack shifted his gaze straight ahead without taking his peripheral vision off the man. He felt the man's eyes follow him. Unnerved, Mack waited for the tram to round a curve then rose and walked to the back of the tram. He kept a sharp watch on the tracks behind.

The tram approached the next station and Mack recognized the busy Bellevue tram station. He made his way back up to his seat before the tram came to a stop. Most passengers disembarked at the busy station and Mack moved up to an empty seat at the front of the tram. He wanted to be closer to the driver for the remainder of his trip. He relaxed when the doors closed and the tram jerked forward.

One kilometer later, the tram rolled into *Tiefenbrunnen* train station. Mack waited for the remaining passengers to exit and stayed close behind them as they walked to the station house. On the far side of the station stood a brightly lit glass and metal building adjacent the train's parking lot. *Spuntino* was written in red neon on the front of the building. The walls were floor-to-ceiling windows. The fluorescent lights inside revealed only a scattering of people inside the restaurant, each sitting alone.

Mack entered and perused the seating area then the bar. Sitting at the back corner of the bar was the heavy-set man from outside the watch store. His salt-and-pepper beard had been trimmed since he'd handed Mack his card and disappeared.

As Mack rounded the bar, the man ignored him, keeping his concentration on the woman standing behind the bar. She was telling him a story in a heavy Swiss German accent Mack didn't understand.

Mack sat on the stool next to him and waited for the woman to stop talking. When she finally took a breath, Mack said, "Herr Schmidt, I presume."

"Excuse me," Herr Schmidt said politely to the woman. He turned to Mack. "Just a second."

He turned back to the woman and said, "This is Mr. Foehrenbacher. Please bring him an espresso and we'll be moving to a table, thank you."

Schmidt grabbed his beer glass and walked through the seating area to a table against the window. He pointed to the seat facing the road running along Lake Zürich. "You sit there." Herr Schmidt sat in the seat across the table and waited for the woman to bring Mack's espresso.

After the woman placed the espresso in front of Mack and left, Herr Schmidt said, "You see the third house on the lake, the one with the high white wall surrounding it?"

Mack looked out the window and nodded.

"That's Keller's house. He spent twenty million renovating it. It's a secure fortress both physically and electronically. You won't need to knock or press any buzzer. When you're at the front door, face the security monitor. If he recognizes you, the door will open automatically. If not, someone will come on the screen and question you." Herr Schmidt took a sip of his beer. "Are you carrying?"

"Yes and I have an extra magazine on me."

Herr Schmidt pulled a small canvas bag from his sport coat pocket, looked over his shoulder than handed it to Mack. "Put it all in this bag and slide it over to me."

Mack hesitated.

"You won't get past Keller's metal detector with a weapon on you."

Mack stuffed the pistol and extra magazine into the bag. He handed it to Herr Schmidt under the table.

Herr Schmidt placed the canvas bag on his lap. "Once inside, you're at the mercy of Keller and his security. They are high paid goons, not smart enough to fear death."

"I thought this was a meeting between Keller and me?"

"It is. Inside his goons will pat you down then disappear. If you're not patted down, find an excuse to leave. If you're followed, either cross the main road and head up the hill or use the lake. The hill is steep and wooded, giving you cover. If you go the hill route, you'll run into motion sensor lights giving away your position. Your best escape is the lake, as long as you can hold your breath for extended periods. Use the neighbors yard to get to the lake then swim toward the city until you see this train station."

Mack downed his espresso in one gulp.

Reading Mack's face, Schmidt said, "Don't worry, it should go fine." His tone was reassuring but not convincing. He added, "Besides, Keller's smart enough not to piss off any of the intel agencies that use his bank."

Mack stood from the table. "Time to do what I gotta do."

"When you finish, I'll be in the parking lot across the street, parked in a blue Mercedes next to the lake," Herr Schmidt said pointing out the window at the lake. Mack pushed his chair back and waited for any final words.

Herr Schmidt turned his attention to the bar, raised and wiggled his near empty beer glass above his head. He winked at the woman behind the counter and raised his chin, gesturing for her to bring him another beer.

$

# CHAPTER 11

Vlad stood in the doorway of the Safari Bar and motioned for Siva and Hilda to stay where they were. He took a step out onto the sidewalk and peered up and down the shadowy street. He eyed every doorway, every crevice and corner. Knowing any professional worth his salt would be unseen, he focused on potential trouble spots, places where, in his previous life, he would wait. He'd reconnoitered situations like this a thousand times before and had only been shot once.

The evening sky was dark blue fading fast to black making it nearly impossible to recognize people on the street. He made out the shapes and focused on the men. The lights in the windows lining the street waned through the pulled shades.

Confident the street was safe, he waved for Hilda and Siva to join him on the sidewalk.

Vlad said, "Stay five paces in front of me. I'll cough if you get too far ahead."

A block later, Siva and Hilda strolled past the long glass wall of the local library. The lights inside shone brightly. A group of teenagers milled around the stacks of books, their faces buried in their phones.

Vlad, five paces behind, looked into the library. *It look like fish bowl with people*, he thought. He refocused his attention on anyone and anything that could be considered a threat. Crowds always hid a threat.

Hilda said, "We turn right at the next alley. The apartment is in the second building on the right." Her voice was barely loud enough for Vlad to hear.

"Stop," Vlad ordered as they entered the alley. He ran up and peered down the street.

Hilda slowed but kept walking. She stopped in front of a gray double door, unzipped a small pocket inside her handbag and lifted out an old skeleton key. She held it up for Vlad to take. "Now you can take the lead."

Vlad wrapped his fingers around the key and let his hand linger for a second, softly touching Hilda's palm.

"I hope I not show you motivation," he said as he slipped the key in the lock. "Stand to side," he added as he swept his left arm behind him.

He pushed open the door, took one step inside and paused. He studied the wide entrance hall then waved for Siva and Hilda to follow.

"We take stairs," Vlad said.

"Since there's no elevator, I guess that makes sense," Hilda replied dryly then patted Vlad on the butt. "The apartment is on the top floor."

They walked up the four stories in silence. At the very top of the stairs there was only one door, a steel reinforced door with two large deadbolt locks.

Hilda took the skeleton key back from Vlad and said, "Siva, give Vlad the apartment keys."

Siva handed the keys to Vlad.

Hilda said, "Do your thing, big guy."

"I have joke for *big* but I not say," Vlad said with a sly grin. "Stay here while I check apartment." He turned and looked at Hilda. The smile on his face vanished. Hilda was holding a Steyr Tactical Machine Pistol with a modified magazine. She pointed the gun at the door.

"In case motivation is needed," Hilda said.

Vlad walked inside, keeping the door ajar.

Hilda stepped to the side, turned and faced the stairs. "You should get against the wall, Siva. Makes you less of a target."

"You *have* been well trained," Siva said.

"After what happened to my mother and brother, my father made sure I could handle myself."

"Can I ask?" Siva said knowing it might touch a nerve.

Hilda showed no emotion. She kept her eyes on the stairs below her. "When I was fourteen, my mother, my little brother Stevie and I were coming back from the grocery store when we were kidnapped at gunpoint by a group of thugs. In exchange for our lives, the kidnappers demanded my father surrender to them. My father agreed as long as he had proof we were still alive. The kidnappers never called him back. They shot my mom and little brother in front of me. I thought I was next and started praying. Then this little man with funny hair walks in, grabs me by the arm and takes me upstairs to a bedroom. By the way the thugs acted toward him, he was definitely the boss. He was carrying a large glass with vodka on ice. He talked incessantly about himself and about how he was about to give me the thrill of my life. In the bedroom, he ripped off my clothes, clamped a shackle attached to a chain around my ankle then pushed me on the bed. He grabbed my hair, pulled my head back and poured vodka down my throat, laughing as poured. Then he crawled on top of me and raped me." Hilda squeezed her eyes shut as the torture tormented her brain once more.

"This went on for a few days. The last time, he was stumbling drunk and couldn't get it up. He passed out so I dug through his pockets, found the key to the shackle, quickly dressed and went into the bathroom. I knew the bedroom door was well guarded so the only way out was through the bathroom window. I was on the second floor so I hung down, dropped to the ground and ran without looking back." Hilda sniffed and wiped the corners of her eyes. "A week later, my father and I found my mom and brother's bodies in an abandoned building. My brother was only five." A tear rolled down her cheek. "We didn't dare go back home. We left with only the clothes on our back and moved around until we settled here. From that day on, I trained every single day for when I find that little prick."

"I'm sorry," Siva said awkwardly.

"Why? You didn't kill my mom or brother or rape me."

Vlad opened the door saving Siva from having to respond.

"Apartment is clean."

Siva walked in and looked around. Against the wall was a sofa flanked by two soft chairs and two standing lamps. A dull red and yellow Persian rug covered most of the linoleum floor. The bare white walls gave the room a sterile feel, like no one lived there.

Hilda closed the door and firmly twisted both deadbolt locks with loud clicks. She tested them to confirm they were locked.

Vlad sat in one of the soft chairs and put the bottle of vodka down on the floor next to him. He slumped back and stuck out his left arm toward the sofa. "You sit here," he said to Hilda.

Siva watched the interaction between Hilda and Vlad and wondered who was tougher. She strolled over and sat in the other chair and faced Vlad.

Hilda lingered then strolled over to Vlad's chair, reached down and grabbed the bottle of vodka off the floor. "I'll put this in the freezer."

Vlad drew in a deep breath through his nose as she walked away. He turned to Siva with a crooked grin on his face. "I not know angels wear perfume."

"You can buy her all the Coco Chanel you want after this is over. Focus on the now."

Vlad's grin disappeared. "I am professional. Nothing get in way of job," he said with such conviction he startled Siva. She recoiled, pushing hard against the chair back.

Hilda strolled back into the room and sat on the sofa. She said, "Why are you helping us, Vlad?"

"This is what I do for living."

"What's the real reason?"

"I owe Mr. Ray Gunn for him saving my father."

Hilda pulled her feet up under her legs. "What did Gunn do?"

"Six month ago, Russian President come to my father and order him to help. My father did not like or trust our President but if he say no, he is killed. So my father say yes. Very soon later, my father meet with President and man named J Otis Weil. I once did work for J Otis Weil and was big mistake. Anyway, they set up bank account in Switzerland and force my father to put in fifty million dollars as payment for protection."

"What bank?" Siva asked.

"Keller Bank in Zürich until it go into a new bank soon to be opened." Vlad answered, looking at

Siva with suspicion. "Why?"

"No reason, go on," Siva said with a flick of her hand.

"The money in bank go missing and President think my father take money back. He not do that. The President order my father to return money or is killed. My father not steal money but President not believe him. Then an American man show up and tell my father there is bomb in car and give him phone number of Mr. Gunn. My father start car with remote switch and car blow up. Mr. Gunn help my father get out of Russia until he safe."

Vlad stood and said, "I need glass water."

Hilda unfolded her legs and pushed herself up. "I'll show you where the glasses are."

A loud boom echoed through the room followed by a blinding flash. The steel reinforced door blew open and hung on its lower hinge. A second later, a man with a black bandana pulled up over his nose swept into the room with a semi-automatic rifle in his hands.

Siva jumped from her chair to run. Before her first step, a bullet tore through her left hip and exited out her right hip. A second bullet hit her left shoulder as she collapsed to the floor.

Vlad grabbed the machine pistol out of Hilda's

hand and shoved her into the kitchen. He turned and fired as a gunman's bullet ripped into his right thigh muscle. He fired the machine pistol hitting the advancing gunman in the throat with flurry of bullets.

As the gunman fell, he continued firing, nicking Vlad's left hand.

Hilda ran across the floor and caught Vlad before he hit the floor. She gently lowered him, examined his hand then his leg wound.

"Go to Siva," Vlad said. He pulled his phone from his pocket, checked to see if it still worked and called emergency. In fluent German, he calmly informed the person on the line there was a shooting and an ambulance was needed immediately.

Hilda yelled out the address as she comforted Siva then screamed in German, "Tell them to hurry, Siva is badly hurt and doesn't look good. She's bleeding pretty bad."

Vlad repeated Hilda's words then pushed himself to his feet. He wobbled as he struggled to get his injured leg under him. When he had his balance, he handed Hilda back her machine pistol and said, "You go, I wait for ambulance. He reached behind his back, took his pistol from his back holster and held it out for Hilda to take."

Siva peered up at Hilda, her breathing labored.

"You and Vlad leave. There could be others."

"Not until the ambulance gets here. Somebody has to let them into the building."

A scream of sirens pierced the night air and grew closer. A few, long minutes later, the intercom buzzed. The shrill voice of authority echoed through the room. "Ambulance, where is the emergency?"

Hilda pressed the intercom button and said, "Top floor," then hurried over to Siva. She pushed the hair from Siva's eyes and wiped the sweat from her forehead. "The ambulance is here. We'll stay if you want."

Siva shook her head. "Find Billy."

Hilda bent over the dead gunman. "He's still breathing... barely. Now he's mumbling something."

Vlad cocked an ear and listened. He raised the machine pistol, clicked it to single shot, took a good look at the gunman, aimed and put a bullet up through the man's chin. "OK, he now dead."

Hilda marched over to Vlad and draped his arm over her shoulder. "There's a doctor not far from here who will treat you without asking questions."

"How do we get out? The police are coming up stairs."

"There's a back staircase through the pantry off

the kitchen. It leads us down to a passage that takes us to an exit a half block from here. The doctor's office is a short walk from there." Hilda looked at Vlad's leg again. "Do you think you can make it?"

"Please get vodka bottle."

Hilda shook her head to show her displeasure as she marched over to the freezer and brought the bottle back to Vlad.

Vlad unscrewed the cap and took a long swallow. He wiped his mouth with his sleeve and said, "Is for pain." He then poured vodka on his leg wound. It took a second before he let out a muted groan. "I no want infection."

As tears pooled in Vlad's eyes, Hilda knew Vlad was in more pain than he was letting on.

Vlad gasped and said, "You lead way, I make it."

As they descended the stairs, Vlad made a call.

"Mr. Gunn, is Vlad. We have problem."

$

# CHAPTER 12

At the bottom of the stairs, Hilda waited for Vlad to brace himself against the wall and finish his call with Ray Gunn.

Vlad ended the call and tried to stand on his own. He faltered and slapped his hand against the wall to catch himself.

Hilda took him by the arm and steadied him. "What did Gunn say?"

"I better go to doctor," Vlad replied, not answering her question. "My head is weak for thinking. I tell you what he say when we at doctor."

Hilda checked the wound in his leg then opened the door a crack and peered into the small courtyard. With the exception of a large oak tree in the middle, the courtyard was empty. She braced herself under Vlad's shoulder and stepped down and out the door. She reached back, gripped the door handle and gently guided the door closed.

In the left corner of the courtyard was a narrow building with maroon shutters. There were two sets of windows on each floor. The building was dark except for the lights in the ground floor windows to the left of the door.

Hilda cradled Vlad with her right arm around his waist, walked him under the tree and over to the door next to the lighted windows. She rapped once on the window, paused then rapped twice. Vlad pulled away from her and limped to the door, nearly falling as he went.

Standing in the doorway was a sickly man with round, wire-rim glasses perched on the end of his nose and wearing in a dirty white smock. He needed a shave and a shower. He pushed his glasses up and looked at Vlad. He shuddered and was about to slam the door shut when Hilda stepped in front of Vlad.

"Dr. Giger, we need your help," Hilda said.

Giger stepped back to let Hilda and Vlad pass.

He lowered his eyes to Vlad's blood-soaked pant leg. "What happened?" he asked.

Hilda guided Vlad into the adjacent room. The small room smelled of ether, burnt hair and cigarettes.

In the middle of the room was a battered patient exam table with padding popping out of holes in the upholstery. Next to it was an instrument stand. Lying in the metal tray were tarnished medical instruments lined up from shortest to longest.

"He was shot in the leg and left hand."

Dr. Giger examined Vlad's leg, front and back. There was no exit wound. "Get up on table," Dr. Giger said to Vlad.

Vlad grimaced as he sat and swung his injured left leg up. "My hand fine, only need bandage to stop bleeding."

Dr. Giger lifted a pair of scissors off the metal tray and cut Vlad's pant leg from the cuff up past his thigh. He dropped the scissors back on the tray and strolled over to the counter behind Vlad. His movements were methodical, learned. It was obvious he'd done this before.

Dr. Giger held a plastic bottle in his right hand and a sterile white cloth in his left. "This will sterilize your wound." He poured clear liquid from the bottle onto the cloth.

"I pour vodka on wound before I come," Vlad said proudly, holding up the bottle of vodka.

"The only way vodka will help you is if you drink it to numb the pain."

Vlad lifted the bottle and took a long pull.

Hilda reached over and took the bottle from Vlad. She took a swig then put the bottle on the counter, out of Vlad's reach. She turned back to Vlad. "No more until this is over." She grasped Vlad's good hand with a reassuring grip.

Dr. Giger patted Vlad's leg wound with the white cloth then wiped away blood.

Vlad clenched Hilda's hand tight. He realized he was hurting Hilda and tried to release his grip.

Hilda didn't let him take his hand away.

Dr. Giger felt around the wound trying to be as gentle as possible as he searched for the bullet. When he finished, he said, "This will hurt. Lie back."

Hilda stood next to Vlad's head as the doctor dug out the bullet. She squeezed his hand with all her strength and asked Vlad questions about Russia, distracting him.

A minute later, the doctor dropped the bloody

bullet on the tray without saying a word. He gingerly pressed thick white gauze on the wound and secured it with medical tape. He lit a cigarette, looked at Hilda and said, "He must rest now. My wife will be here in a few minutes and she can clean his leg and treat the wound. That will buy him some time." Giger vacuumed in a deep drag off his cigarette. "He must go to hospital as soon as he can."

"We don't have that option right now," Hilda said.

Vlad pulled Hilda close. "I rest here for little while. If there is problem, I go myself to hospital. You find Billy Mack then call me."

Hilda kissed Vlad on the cheek, thanked Dr. Giger and hurried out. Vlad watched her through the window as she strode through the courtyard and out of sight.

Inside Peter and Hilda's secret apartment, the paramedics carried Siva down the four flights of stairs swiftly and steadily.

During the two-minute ride to the University Hospital, one of the paramedics worked diligently on her hips to suppress the bleeding.

In the emergency room, a team of doctors moved around Siva with frenzied yet choreographed movements, examining her. One nurse was taking a vile of blood from Siva's right arm while another listened to her heart. A third nurse had attached electrodes to various points on Siva's body and was adjusting the monitor over her head.. A young doctor finally found a vein in Siva's left arm an inserted a needle attached to a long, plastic tube filled with plasma.

To Siva, everything in the room was moving in slow motion. She heard echoed voices coming from the doctors and nurses as they moved around her but did not understand a word. They were speaking their own language.

Siva's attention diverted to a nurse who leaned in and said, "Stay with us." The nurse smiled reassuringly as she wiped Siva's forehead with a cool, moist towel. Siva smiled back or at least thought she did.

The light in the room dimmed as she watched the doctors walk away talking quietly. She closed her eyes and thought of Billy.

$

# CHAPTER 13

Mack walked out the glass doors of the *Spuntino* restaurant, waited for a city bus heading to the train station to pass then jogged across the busy street to the sidewalk running along the lake.

The wind blew in off Lake Zürich. As Mack hoofed it down the sidewalk heading to Keller's house, all five of his senses on high alert. Staying as best he could in the shadows, he zeroed in on the darkness around him. His ears listened for ominous sounds and his eyes probed for sinister movements. The rustling of the trees forced him to heighten each of his senses.

The cars on the street raced past, speeding up as they left the Zürich city limits. Approaching Keller's house, Mack tuned his ears to the sound of the tires on the asphalt. He imagined what the sound would be like if a car jumped the curb and came up on the sidewalk behind him.

He reached Keller's front gate and stood in front of the security screen. A few seconds later, the gate slid open, wide enough for Mack to slip through. Walking up to the house, Mack heard the gate behind him rapidly slide shut and lock with a prison cell clank.

A light above the front door flickered then illuminated, calling Mack toward it.

Keller's front door swung open. A large man filled the doorway. He wore a tight fitting white dress shirt with shirt sleeves that were bursting at the seams. A thick gold chain hung around his neck. His spiked hair was dyed a brilliant white and was translucent under the light.

The man vigorously patted Mack down. When he finished, he scoffed at Mack then stood close in order to intimidate him. "Down the hall and to your left," he said with a sneer.

Mack squeezed by and confidently strolled down the hall memorizing the layout as he went.

He walked into a large, high-ceilinged room overlooking Lake Zürich. The room was sparsely yet expensively furnished. Mack figured the few pieces of furniture in the room were worth more than what most people earn in a year. On the wall hung two Van Gogh paintings. Mack assumed they were originals.

Keller stood across the room. He peered out the tall windows overlooking the lake, a glass in his hand. Without turning around, he said, "Welcome Mr. McMillan. Let's not waste time with small talk as if we're interested in getting to know each other. You're here representing Siva Afari and your organization. I'm here to get my $100 million back."

"It's not *your* money."

"That's true but I treat every dollar, euro or franc on account in my bank as mine." Keller took a sip of his drink. "It's how I guarantee my clients the best possible security."

"Well, you failed with Ms. Afari. She'd like to know what you're doing to retrieve her money."

"It's not her money, we both know that. But it is money entrusted to me. That being said, our system has evidence she misappropriated or should I say *borrowed* the money and we believe you are involved."

Mack paused, more for affect. He walked over to the windows and stood next to Keller. He smelled the scotch whiskey in Keller's glass.

"Beautiful view especially on a moonlit night like tonight." Mack said and tapped the window. "I assume this glass is bullet-proof."

"The best money can buy."

"It's probably sufficient if a common criminal takes a shot at you." Mack grinned knowing Keller could see his reflection in the window. "If a real player wanted in, your bullet proof glass will only slow him down a second or two."

"Enough time for me to get to safety." Keller replied then turned and faced Mack. "You're not here to admire my windows, you're here because your bosses want their money back. I agreed to meet with you because I also want to get the money back. Since our interests are mutual and, if you say Ms. Afari and you didn't abscond with the money, tell me what you know and I will return the favor. But, I won't violate Swiss banking secrecy laws."

Mack kept his eyes looking out at the lake and said, "We know Ms. Afari's money was taken without her consent or approval. Your bank is responsible for her money and we expect it back. That is what we know... as of now."

"I'm disappointed. I thought your organization had better resources, better intelligence."

Mack caught a flicker of light in the middle of the lake. It was a feint flash and far off. He studied the lake and made out the silhouette of a fishing boat sitting about a quarter mile offshore. He turned his attention back to Keller's reflection in the window.

"A hundred million doesn't just disappear, Mr. Keller. I was led to believe Keller Bank, the bank you own, has the best security and the proper checks and balances. That tells me someone inside your bank is involved, either directly or indirectly."

"All of my employees are properly vetted and I am running a thorough investigation. As of right now, we believe someone inside your organization or your sister organization in Jerusalem masterminded the theft."

"So you know who funded the account."

"Yes, and I'm smart enough not to get on the wrong side of either organization. If someone in my bank is involved, and that's not likely, they were coerced into cooperating by someone from within your organizations. Are you looking inside your own houses?"

Mack didn't like where conversation was headed. He had to find a credible excuse to gather his thoughts while keeping the door open for him to return. He fished his phone from his pocket. "Before I say anything more, I need to make a call. Is there somewhere private?"

"Back down the hall in the foyer near the front door."

Mack strolled down the hall, counting the rooms with closed doors. He examined the locks on each door as he strolled past.

The large man dressed in white stood in the foyer next to the front door.

"Go tell your boss he wants you," Mack said as he flicked his thumb over his shoulder.

"Fuck you," the large man mumbled as he left.

Mack held the phone to his ear pretending to be on a call. He walked over to the first door on the left side and pushed down on the handle. The door opened to an opulent bathroom with a gold sink and toilet. High above the toilet was a transom window with double-paned glass.

Mack stood on the toilet and looked out the narrow, rectangular window. A few feet away stood the upper section of the thick stone wall guarding Keller's house. Mack tested the window latch without opening the narrow window.

He stepped down off the toilet, turned and opened the door.

Blocking the doorway was the large man, glaring

down at him. "What the fuck are you doing?"

"What do you think I was doing in here?"

The big man kept his glare on Mack.

"I was going to squirt but decided the toilet was too nice," Mack answered and squeezed past the man and into the hallway. He didn't look back as he walked away.

Keller stood with his back to the windows facing Mack as he strolled back into the room.

The lights in the room began flashing and a high-pitched siren cut through the air. Floodlights suddenly lit up the yard leading to the lake. A group of men rushed up from the lake firing automatic rifles at Mack and Keller. The bullets bounced off the glass, leaving large nicks and small cracks. A thick metal shutter dropped down and clanked when it hit the ground. The shutter shook as the barrage of bullets pinged off the metal.

Keller sprinted past Mack and down the hall.

Mack turned to see Keller and the large bodyguard run into a room halfway down the hall and slam the door.

Mack hurried after them. At the door, he heard muffled voices coming from inside. He pounded on the door.

The small video screen next to the door lit up and showed Keller's face inside a panic room. "You're on your own, Mr. McMillan." The video screen went dark.

Mack sprinted to the bathroom near the front door and hurried inside. He locked the door knowing it was a useless gesture.

A blast reverberated through the house. The concussion of the explosion violently shook the entire bathroom. Water shot out the faucet so hard it splashed onto the floor.

Mack pressed his ear against the door and listened. He heard multiple footsteps crunching on shattered glass followed by a commanding voice Mack took to be Eastern Europe. A litany of voices responded quickly.

The voices grew closer, not worried about being heard. Mack tried to determine what exact language they were speaking. It sounded Slavic, Russian or Ukrainian.

Mack had to find a way out, a way to safety. His first instinct was to make a run for the front door.

The voices inside the house drew closer, making his decision easy. Without another thought, he stepped up on the toilet, turned the latch on the transom then pulled himself up. He thanked his parents for his slim frame and crawled through the narrow window. He jockeyed his legs until he stood on the windowsill then jumped across the open space. He grabbed the top of the stone wall and hung on with his fingers. Paying no mind to the cuts and scrapes on his fingers, he steadied himself before mustering the strength to pull his body up. He sat atop the wall and wiped the blood from his fingers onto his pant leg.

He heard the sound of splintering wood and realized the bathroom door had been kicked in. A few seconds later, deliberate voices hurried out the front door giving positions and status updates. Mack swung his leg over the outside of the wall, hung down then dropped to the hard ground and rolled into the neighbors yard.

He jumped to his feet, froze and listened. Voices filled the street behind him. There was only one way for him to go. He crouched, snuck along the wall and made his way to the lake.

He silently slid into the chilly water, careful not to cause ripples. The water was quickly up to his neck and he slowly swam over and under the nearby dock. At the end of the dock, he planned out his route back toward the city and looked around for what to avoid. He had to get past Keller's house without being seen.

The thick rubber raft that brought the attackers ashore was pulled up onto Keller's yard. A lone gunman stood next to it with his eyes focused on Keller's house.

Mack sucked in a deep breath, sunk under the water and swam away from shore, kicking with everything he had. It was nearly impossible to see in the dark water. He held his breath for over a minute, then painfully surfaced, rolled over and stuck his mouth and nose out of the water. He inhaled deeply. With his ears under water he heard only muffled voices before submerging even deeper. He rolled back over and swam vigorously away from shore. He repeated this for the next 10 minutes before he dared pop his head out of the water for a look.

The rubber raft was no longer on the lawn. He turned his eyes left and saw the raft slowly patrolling along the shore. A searchlight skimmed the water. Mack sunk down until his eyes were just above water level. The boat turned sharply left and motored toward him. He lowered his head and began pushing his arms up with every ounce of strength in him. As he descended, he kept his eyes on the surface and thanked the Lord for Lake Zürich being a deep lake.

He watched the rubber raft motor over him and head for the center of the lake. He started to gag from lack of oxygen. He struggled to hold his breath for another thirty seconds, counting off in his head.

At the surface, he emerged to see the raft stop and wait for an approaching fishing boat. The lights of the fishing boat scanned the water around it.

Mack turned and swam toward shore. Twenty yards from land he stopped and studied the shoreline. Clear. He silently dog paddled to shore.

He made his way up to a clump of trees along the shoreline and caught his breath. After a minute, he walked along the shore until he came to the small park across the street from the train station. He crouched behind a tree, brushed his wet hair back and looked for Herr Schmidt's blue Mercedes.

The car was parked in a dark corner on the far side of the parking lot, close to the water. Mack used the line of trees running along the shore as cover until he was thirty yards from the car. He was close enough to see inside the car.

He made out two people sitting inside the car.

"Damn." He took a knee behind a tree. It was decision time. Did he approach the car unarmed or find his way back to Peter?

$

# CHAPTER 14

Mack studied the two silhouettes sitting in the blue Mercedes. They sat motionless, facing forward, peering out the windshield. For a brief second, Mack thought they were store mannequins. Then the driver put his hand on the steering wheel.

Mack moved closer.

The larger of the two was a broad-shouldered bearded man and Mack figured it to be Herr Schmidt as planned. The other silhouette was a small female with shoulder length hair.

She turned, faced Schmidt and began lecturing

him. Schmidt nodded the entire time she spoke, keeping his eyes forward.

When they went back to peering out the windshield, Mack worked his way around the park and behind the car. He came up to the back window behind the driver's seat and breathed a sigh of relief when he recognized Hilda. Then it hit him. *What was she doing here? Something went wrong.*

He opened the back door and jumped in. The ceiling light did not illuminate.

"Why are you here, Hilda?" Mack asked.

"Why are you soaking wet?" Hilda replied, her tone flat.

"I ran into a little problem at Keller's house."

Mack explained the raid, Keller hiding inside his panic room and his own escape through the bathroom window. When he finished, he added, "The strange thing was they didn't make a concerted effort to find me. They went through the motions but took off quickly back to their boat out on the lake."

Herr Schmidt said, "Keller has the latest in security. You can bet the attackers were on a clock knowing exactly how much time they had."

Hilda nodded and said, "Were they after you or Keller... or both of you?"

Mack shivered from his wet clothes and rubbed both his arms. "It's the second time someone's come after me so I have to assume it's me."

"Don't be so sure," Hilda replied. "The man at the Brasserie was shot and killed, not you or Siva."

"True, but it's safer if I assume I was the target here."

Herr Schmidt loudly cleared his throat as he glanced at Hilda.

Hilda turned in her seat. "Billy, Siva was shot and is in the hospital."

Mack stared blankly at her.

"She was hit in the hip and is in surgery right now."

Mack stared out at the lake, his mind spinning.

"What happened? Where the hell was Vlad? Wait, how did anybody know you were there? I thought the apartment was a well-kept secret." Billy said, his cadence unrelenting.

"Good question. The gunman came in, zeroed in on Siva and fired. She was definitely the target. Luckily, Vlad instantly reacted and saved Siva's life."

"How can you be sure Siva was the target? What in the hell-"

"Calm down Billy," Hilda said firmly.

"Don't tell me to calm down. What in the hell went wrong?"

Hilda calmly explained the shoot out at the apartment, the ambulance and Vlad's visit with the doctor. She kept her eyes on Mack while he gazed out at the lake.

"How in the hell did anyone know you were there?"

"I don't know."

A full two minutes of silence filled the car. No one dared say a word.

Mack finally brought his eyes back to Hilda. "Is Siva going to... Sorry, are Siva and Vlad both going to be ok?"

Hilda expelled a long, full breath. "Honestly... Vlad will be fine but it's too early to tell for Siva."

"Take me to her."

"We can do that but she will be in surgery for a few hours, if not more. You won't be able to see her."

"How the hell do you know that?"

"My dad spoke with Ray Gunn. The hospital is

keeping Gunn updated and he's arranging for someone to be at the hospital to protect her when she comes out of surgery. While Siva is in surgery, Gunn is organizing a team to protect her twenty-four seven while she recovers and recuperates."

Mack squeezed his lips together with his fingers, thinking of his response. He fought to keep his temper in check.

"Billy, it makes more sense for us to figure out who is after her and you and why. That's the best thing for Siva right now." Hilda said. She gave Schmidt a look telling him to back her up.

"She's right Billy. If you don't, you'll both be looking over your shoulders for the rest of your lives and they will be most likely short lives."

"My father is waiting for us at the Safari Bar. He's taking a big risk exposing himself to help you."

"I need some air," Mack said then climbed out of the car and walked to the lakeshore. The reflection of the city lights flickered off the water.

Hilda and Herr Schmidt quickly joined him. They stood next to him in silence knowing no words would be of comfort.

Herr Schmidt handed Mack the canvas bag with the Colt .45 and extra magazine inside.

Mack turned away from the water. He grinned and gazed off into the distance with resolve. He said, "I played baseball with a pitcher named Cam Killebrew. Off the field, Cam was the calmest, gentlest guy you'd ever meet, wouldn't hurt a soul. As soon as he stepped on the pitcher's mound though, he was nasty, the most competitive ballplayer I ever knew. He had a dominating arm and put the ball where he wanted. When someone hit a home run off him, the next time that guy came to the plate, Cam nailed him in the back with a bruising fastball. Then he'd look over at me with a cockeyed smile and say, 'Don't get mad, get even.' After that, every time that batter came to the plate he struckout."

Mack looked inside the bag and his grin vanished.

"Time to get even."

$

# CHAPTER 15

Vlad sat in the examination room wondering where Dr. Giger went. He'd left ten minutes ago but the searing pain in Vlad's right leg made it seem like hours. He was about to climb down off the examination table when a frail woman walked in.

"I am Frau Giger. Lie back down, this will only take a few minutes."

Frau Giger meticulously cleaned and dressed Vlad's leg wound and when she finished, took a warm cloth and washed Vlad's face.

"Do you want me to give you something for the

pain?" she asked.

"Only if it not slow me."

"You will be a bit groggy for a couple hours."

"Then I not take."

"Suit yourself but you need to stay off that leg for a couple hours," she said as she toweled off the sweat from his forehead.

"I take pain. Is not problem for me," Vlad said with a grimace then closed his eyes.

"It is not about the pain. You may further injure your leg. It is better you sleep," she said as she gently lifted Vlad's left hand, then numbed it with a spray, sewed in four stitches and tied the thread off. She wrapped thin gauze around his hand, securing it with white medical tape.

She handed him a pair of pants. "These will be a little big, but will do the job."

Thirty minutes later, Vlad woke with a jerk. He howled and grabbed his thigh to strangle the pain. After a minute, the pain subsided and he fished his phone from his pocket.

He didn't wait for an answer before saying, "Mr. Gunn, Vlad speaking. I am in doctor office and Hilda gone to find Billy Mack. She is to call me when she with him."

"I know. How is your leg?"

"I live. I call you because I forget to tell you something. Before I shoot man in apartment, he was talking to himself and he speaking Russian but with Ukrainian accent. There is Ukrainian gang that work for Russian government. This gang sell girls for sex and give Russian President part of money they make. They also kill enemies of Russian President."

"Good to know. What else can you tell me about the gunman or his gang?"

"The gang is paid by a company owned by friend of President. You know him. His name J Otis Weil. He is sneaky little shit, yes?"

"You don't have to tell me. I should have figured Weil was involved. Among his many depravities, he bankrolls the sex trafficking for the Russian mafia."

"He is banker for Russian President and his friends."

"I will make some calls, pull in a few favors. Now, in our previous talk, I asked you to think about how that gunman knew you were in the apartment?"

"I think of but not know how man know."

"That's important for us to know. It will point us in the right direction to finding out who is after Siva."

"Is good idea to know. I go to hospital and wait for Siva to finish surgery. Maybe she have idea."

"She may be unconscious for a day or two but, if your leg is up to it, I want you to go to the hospital and stay with her, keep her safe."

Vlad gingerly stepped down from the examination table and limped to the door hoping his leg would make it to the hospital. Dr. and Frau Giger were nowhere to be found so he quietly opened the door and stepped outside into the empty courtyard.

Vlad walked back to *Zähringerstrasse* wincing with each step. He passed the bright lights of the library, staying near the building walls as he kept a vigilant eye out. He hoped a taxi would drive by.

The ache in his leg became more tolerable as he approached the Safari Bar. He walked by the bar without looking inside. A few steps later, he felt a hand on his shoulder. He gripped the machine pistol in coat pocket and calmly turned around.

A tall man with long gray hair let go of Vlad's shoulder and said, "My name is Peter. I'm Hilda's father. Before you go to the hospital, come inside the bar."

Vlad released his grip on the machine pistol and followed Peter inside.

Hilda sat at the same table as earlier in the

evening. Billy Mack sat next to her in damp clothing.

Hilda winked at Vlad and said, "This is Billy Mack. He's Siva's friend. Someone is also after Mr. Mack and I think it's the same crew after Siva."

Mack stood and extended his hand, "Nice to see you again, Vlad."

Vlad gripped Mack's hand firmly. "Same for me. I think you are man who like trouble."

"Am I missing something?" Hilda asked.

"You might say I introduced Vlad to Ray Gunn and let's leave it at that," Mack said and looked at Peter for help.

Peter leaned down and kissed his daughter on the forehead. "When this is over, I'll fill you in. For now, I'm going back to my office to make calls. I know people who know people... if you know what I mean. When I learn anything, I will pass on that information." Peter turned, walked down the back hallway and disappeared out the door and into a dark alley.

"What he mean, 'know people who know people?'" Vlad asked.

"Whenever a crew is hired, word gets on the street. My father once worked with people who, how do I put this, hear things and for the right price will tell you."

"I know who after Siva," Vlad said. "The man I kill was part of Russian-Ukrainian gang, *The Mogils*. They work for Russian President."

"*The Mogils?*"

"That is nickname for *The Mogilschiiki*, which in Russian mean 'gravediggers.'"

"How do you know he was *Mogils*?" Mack asked.

"He have tattoo of two snakes wrapped around stick on left hand. That is symbol of *Mogils*."

"Do you mean they're assassins?" Hilda asked.

Vlad nodded. "They also take girls and sell them for having sex."

"What I should know about *The Mogils*?" Mack asked.

"They mainly from city of Kharkiv in Ukraine and are former communists who want Ukraine go back to Russia. They make money killing enemies of Russia in Ukraine and Europe. They make other money for bringing young girls to Europe and America for having sex. They kill anyone who get in way."

"Prostitutes?" Hilda asked.

Vlad nodded.

Mack took a long hard look at Vlad. "Who runs *The Mogils*?"

Vlad said, "Many years ago, maybe seven, eight years, the leaders of *Mogils* were killed by someone inside organization. No one know who. There was power struggle for one year and man named Sergei Vukovic become leader. He was very bad man. Even Russian President afraid of him. Last year he is found in hotel room in Kiev with throat cut and knife stuck in chest. The Ukrainian police very happy he dead and rule he dead by suicide."

"Who is the leader of the *Mogils* now?" Mack asked.

"That I not know. Even people close to *Mogils* not know."

"What do you know?"

"I know Russian President give orders to *Mogils* but you never prove he involved. He have man who tell *Mogils* what President order and where to putting girls in Europe. That man J Otis Weil. My father tell me J Otis have office in Zurich for getting money. I once work with him but he not pay me and try to kill me." Vlad's eyes tightened. "When I see J Otis, I kill him."

"Get in line," Mack said. "If J Otis Weil is here

in Zürich, he's up to something bad. The only way to get to him is to find out who *The Mogils* are working with here in Zürich. The question is where do we start?"

"Follow the money," Hilda said. "We start at the source, the bank."

"Keller Bank," Mack replied, nodding.

"Who at the bank?" Hilda asked.

"Keller was reluctant to tell me anything about the missing money. He believes someone inside the CIA or Mossad skirted the bank's security and took the money."

"Yeah, right," Hilda said.

"I think he believes that."

Hilda hooked her hair behind her ears. "Who at the bank has access to Siva's account?"

"Besides Keller, most likely Siva's account manager, someone in IT security or the head of technology. They're the most likely."

"Then that's where we start," Mack said. "We pay a visit to Siva's account manager first. She told me his name is Marek Gullberg."

Vlad stood to go. "Where this banker live?"

Hilda pulled out her phone and tapped the screen a few times. She looked up at Vlad. "You're going to the hospital as planned. I have a ride on its way to take you there."

Vlad opened his mouth to say something.

Hilda wagged her finger. "This is not open for discussion. You go to the hospital to watch over Siva *and* while you're there, have your leg checked."

Mack sat silent. Anything he said would go over like a Red Sox fan cheering at Yankee Stadium. He looked out the front windows to see a taxi idling out on the street.

Hilda stood and helped Vlad to the front entrance.

When she returned, she asked, "How do we find Marek Gullberg?"

"We ask your father."

$

# CHAPTER 16

Mercy Geissel strolled sluggishly out of Keller Bank as if she were heading home after a demanding day of work. She skirted the left side of *Paradeplatz* and made her way to the taxi stand around the corner. She discreetly scanned the area as she approached a lone taxi idling next to the curb. She opened the back door and glanced back at street leading to Keller Bank. She knew that if professionals were following her, she'd have no clue.

She gave the taxi driver her destination then slumped down in her seat as the taxi drove away from *Paradeplatz*.

After the taxi crossed the Sihl River and turned north, Geissel leaned forward and said, "I'm sorry, I was just texted a new address for my dinner. It's at the restaurant *Cantinetta Antinori*. Do you know it?"

"Of course," the taxi driver said, looking at her in the rearview mirror. "But the restaurant is on *Augustinergasse*. I can only get you near the restaurant."

"That is fine," Geissel answered then leaned back in her seat with a sly smile on her face. The taxi driver now had to take a roundabout way and drop her off at spot near *Bahnhofstrasse*, the main shopping street in Zürich.

*If anyone was following her*, she thought, *I can lose them on Bahnhofstrasse*.

The taxi pulled to a stop next to a small square leading to *Bahnhofstrasse*. She handed him fifty Francs and stepped out of the taxi without thanking him.

In the middle of the square stood a modern art sculpture that looked like gray marble Legos trying to imitate Stonehenge. Geissel raised her eyes in mock disgust as she walked around the sculpture.

*Bahnhofstrasse* was crowded with shoppers, tourists and straggling businessmen making their way home from a long day at the office.

Geissel perused the street then weaved through a group of tourists and crossed the street. She put her head down and marched up *Augustinergasse* heading toward a dark green medieval building with maroon trim. *Cantinetta Antinori* was written in neon above the front door.

She studied the glass window on front door to see if anyone was behind her. Satisfied she wasn't being followed she pushed her way into the restaurant.

She slid through the heavy curtains inside the front door and walked through the restaurant to the back stairs. At the top of the stairs, she veered left and headed to the upstairs dining room. Every table in the room was filled with well-dressed customers.

J Otis Weil sat at a table for two in the far corner. Next to him stood a silver wine bucket on a stand. The wine bottle in the stand was upside down.

Geissel smiled diplomatically as she approached the table.

Seeing her, J Otis lifted his glass, took a swig then stood and stepped toward her.

Geissel awkwardly stuck out her hand.

J Otis took her hand then kissed her on her cheek as if they were close friends. When he pulled away, he snapped his fingers at the waiter and pointed to the wine bucket.

Geissel had no intention of engaging in small talk. She sat, pulled her chair in and said, "Mr. Weil, I normally conduct bank business in my office." Her voice was deliberately loud enough so the nearby tables heard.

"Please Mercy, call me J Otis," he replied then lowered his voice, "And the business we'll discuss has nothing to do with Keller Bank and my account."

"You no longer have an account at Keller Bank."

J Otis eyed the waiter approaching the table with another bottle of wine and held his hand up for Geissel to stop talking.

The waiter held the bottle in front of J Otis so he could read the label, then uncorked it and poured a small amount of white wine in a new glass.

J Otis took a sip of the wine, sloshed it around in his mouth then stared off into the distance. After a short pause, he swallowed and nodded at the waiter.

The waiter poured a small amount into Geissel's glass without asking. He turned and filled J Otis' glass nearly to the brim.

J Otis raised his glass and said, "To my new bank."

Geissel clinked glasses, glared at J Otis and put her glass down without taking a drink.

J Otis furrowed his brow. "What?"

"I want my money returned."

"It's not your money."

"I was entrusted with it so I treat it as mine."

J Otis took a long drink of his wine. "Don't go down that path."

"Nevertheless, you came to me to set up untraceable accounts and I went to great lengths to do that. If the authorities find out, I'm the one who goes to jail. For me to stick my neck out like that, we agreed the Sunden Capital account was to be kept open and funded for a minimum of six months or until I secured my place running Keller Bank. You gave me your word."

J Otis gulped down the remainder of his wine then licked his lips. He said, "In business, circumstances change and you make the necessary adjustments. I was able to raise the necessary capital for my bank six months quicker than anticipated. My partners, my investors expect my bank to be operating as soon as it is funded. There is no reason for me to delay. I have deals that require funding next week. I won't tell you what happens to anyone who gets in the way of those deals."

"We had an agreement." Geissel replied and folded her arms across her chest.

"We never agreed on any dates."

Geissel knew she had lost the argument. She tried one more angle. "You agreed to keep the money in Keller Bank until I had what I wanted and I..." Geissel pounded her finger against her chest, "...I agreed to release the money. I demand the account be reopened for another three months."

"I held up my end of the agreement," J Otis said. "In fact, I over performed my part of the bargain. Because of me, you were promoted to second in command at the bank, with a hefty pay raise, I might add."

Geissel dropped her hands into her lap. "This was never about money, my job or my career. You should have figured that out when I turned down your offer to join your new bank."

The waiter appeared with two menus in his hand. He refilled J Otis' wine glass before handing a menu to J Otis. Before he could hand the other menu to Geissel, J Otis handed back his menu and said, "We will both have the *scaloppini*, thank you."

When the waiter was out of earshot, Geissel said, "I don't eat meat."

"Then just eat the noodles that come with it.

That way, we can finish this discussion and move on to other things." J Otis winked at her then downed his wine glass and poured himself another.

"That isn't happening." Geissel said stone-faced. "The only reason I slept with you was to get what I wanted and what you promised. You still haven't delivered."

"You need patience, Mercy. I have everything under control."

"I'm done being patient. You haven't lived up to your end of our agreement."

"Neither have you."

Geissel stood and pushed in her chair. "This isn't over."

"Sit down, enjoy our dinner together. Later we can see what comes up... it will be *me* of course." J Otis laughed uncontrollably.

$

# CHAPTER 17

Mercy Geissel sat in the back seat and stared out the car window at the choppy waters of Lake Zürich. The lights from the city's skyline mirrored off the rippling water, distorting the reflection. She felt as if she were looking at a Van Gogh painting.

She tried to erase J Otis from her mind. The mere thought of him grated on her. She wanted to take a shower and wash him off. She struggled to put the encounter with J Otis behind her as she peered out the window. It wasn't like her to let anyone, especially someone like J Otis, get to her.

She forced herself to get back to the task at hand and turned her attention to the woman sitting to her left.

The woman wore a plain gray blouse, navy blue corduroy slacks and black soft sole shoes. Her oval face had no distinguishing characteristics. Her brown, shoulder-length hair was neatly brushed. She was the type of person you pass without noticing. That was her intention. She worked hard at not being noticed.

"What happened?" Geissel spurted out.

"I missed, kind of." The woman replied.

Geissel realized the driver was listening and lowered her voice. "Take care of it tonight."

"It will be, but this is now a two person job. I've brought in my best and he's already on it," the woman answered. "Unless you want to tell me how to do my job."

Geissel wasn't about to argue with her. "Take care of it tonight."

"I won't miss this time."

"When we get inside," Geissel said, "let me do all the talking. Keller doesn't handle stress well. When he sees you, he may panic."

Geissel pressed the button on the armrest

activating the microphone imbedded in the roof above her and said, "Park as close as you can to Mr. Keller's front entrance."

The driver nodded then eased up on the gas pedal. He gently nudged the car up on the curb and stopped with the back passenger door close to the mansion's front entrance.

"Stay here, we won't be long," Geissel said to the driver as she stepped out of the car followed by the plain-looking woman.

"Stand out of view of the camera," Geissel said to the woman.

Geissel stood to the right of the entrance, very close in front of the security panel. She tapped the small screen and leaned into the lens to make sure her face dominated the pinhole camera.

Geissel heard a loud click and the solid front gate slowly slid open. She strolled in and motioned for the woman to hurry. They paused to study Keller's mansion while waiting for the gate to close and lock.

"Stay close behind me," Geissel said.

She marched up to the front door and fidgeted as she impatiently waiting for someone to open the door. The door opened a crack and she saw half of Keller's face, his right eye scanned her up and down.

Keller pulled the door open, staying behind it and out of sight.

"Hurry," he said.

When Geissel hesitated, Keller reached around the door and yanked her into the house by her arm. He quickly grabbed the door handle to slam the door and stopped cold.

"What the hell," Keller shrieked and pulled his arm away. "What is she doing here?"

"I called her," Geissel said forcefully. "If we want resolve this disaster fast, Bella is needed."

Keller looked over at Bella, trying to hide the fear in his eyes. "I didn't authorize this."

Bella gave Keller an ambiguous smile.

It was the first time Keller had ever seen Bella smile, if that's what it was.

"Follow me," Keller replied and walked down the hall.

Keller strode into his living room and abruptly stopped. Geissel bumped into him then stepped to his side.

The floor in Keller large living room was covered with shattered glass. Two enormous floor-to-ceiling windows overlooking the lake had been blown out. There was a large hole in the metal shutter.

Geissel slowly rotated to assess the damage. The wall behind her was peppered with bullet holes. Keller's priceless Van Gogh had two large holes in the middle of the yellow vase. Geissel had often wondered if the painting was the original or a forgery. If it was a forgery, she was certain Keller wouldn't know the difference.

"What happened here?"

Keller walked across the floor, the soles of his shoes crunching on the shattered bits of glass as he went. He stood in the huge gap where the window used to be.

"When I met with Billy Mack to find out what he knew about the missing money, I was attacked."

"By whom?" Bella asked.

"I have no idea. There was an explosion blowing out my windows and I saw a team of men rushing toward me. I was greatly outnumbered so Roman, my bodyguard, rushed me into my panic room." Keller studied Bella's face. He was beginning to think Geissel did the right thing bringing in Bella earlier than he wanted.

"You were lucky," Bella said as she bent down and picked up a shard of glass. She ran her finger across the flat side and studied the tip of her finger. She touched her fingertip to her tongue to taste it.

"This was military-grade C4."

"What does that mean?" Keller asked.

"Whoever attacked was either military or had access to military-grade C4. Did you get a look at them?"

Keller shook his head. "They were wearing black ski masks. I was able to see them on the security camera screen in my panic room. Two of the attackers had long hair, down their backs."

"That rules out military," Bella said. She tossed the shard of glass on the floor. "How long were you in the panic room?"

Keller shrugged and said, "When the alarm system alerted me it was safe, I emerged to find this." He swept his arm around the room.

Geissel tiptoed across the floor trying to avoid the shards of glass. "Why would commandos invade your house and attack you?"

"Commandos?"

"Whatever they were. Why would they go after you?"

"Why do you think? The missing money, of

course." Keller peered up at the stars. "What I can't figure out is how they knew I was going to be here. I don't normally get home until much later."

"It wasn't you they were after."

Keller turned and faced Geissel, a perplexed look on his face. "You think they were after Billy Mack and not me?"

"There's no other logical explanation. Mack and Siva Afari stole the money and the intel agencies want it back. They sent the team of commandos."

"I'm not so sure. Mack was determined to find the missing money. I got the impression he has a good idea who is behind the missing money."

"He was lying, playing you."

"I think you're wrong about that. But if he was playing me, he did a masterful job of it. Better than any actor."

"How come you don't believe me? Mack is a spy, that's what spies do for a living. They lie, cheat, steal and then convince you they're on your side."

"His actions were different then the spies we normally deal with. That's what struck me as odd with him. He was different, he acted different."

"That's because he's very good at what he does. What did he tell you?"

"We didn't get that far. The explosion and the invaders ended our conversation."

"When you were in your panic room, did Mack say anything about the men that attacked you?"

"He wasn't in the panic room."

"Really?" Geissel paused. "Don't you find that odd? Perhaps he arranged the attack? Did you ever think of that?"

Keller shrugged his shoulders. "The last I saw of him, he was running toward the front door and away from the attackers."

Geissel paused then asked, "Did the commandos take him?"

"I have no idea."

"How about Roman, maybe he knows where Mack is."

"Roman knows only what I know. Besides, I sent him home. He should be back in the morning."

"Do you think that's wise given what happened here?"

"The cops have come and gone and I'm not staying here tonight. I've booked a room at the Dolder Hotel in their VIP section where no one is allowed in without security clearing them."

Geissel walked out onto the patio. She waved for Keller to join her.

Keller hesitated before taking tentative steps. He stood next to Geissel.

"When our parents were murdered why did you take me and my sister in?"

"Why are you asking that now?"

"Since you don't believe me about Mack, I am beginning to think you don't trust me and that leads me to wonder why you took us in. Was it just to groom me, as you like to call it? Was that why you really wanted me, for sex?"

Keller winced. "I don't recall you complaining."

"I didn't have much of a choice." Geissel stepped close to Keller. "And why did you basically ignore my sister?"

"She scared me. She scared a lot of people."

"Well, that's water under the bridge now. Let's go upstairs and get you packed for the Dolder."

Walking across the shattered glass, Keller said, "Call Khandelwal and tell him I want to see him in my office first thing in the morning."

"Tomorrow's Saturday and Lee doesn't work on weekends."

"Then I'll go visit him at his house."

"What can Lee tell you about the missing money?" Bella asked as she took Keller by the elbow and led him down the hall.

"He's following the trail of the money from the time it left my bank."

"Are you telling us Lee knows where the money is?" Geissel asked.

"He told me he'd know everything by tomorrow morning latest."

"That's great news," Geissel said.

"Just in case, when I get to the Dolder, I'm calling Khandelwal, see what he's learned so far."

"You go upstairs and throw an overnight bag together. Bella will go with you, keep you company just in case. While you're packing, I will call Lee to see what he's learned and tell him to meet you at the Dolder tomorrow."

"Fine, but I want him at the Dolder tomorrow morning, first thing."

"You're the boss," Geissel said with a soothing smile.

$

# CHAPTER 18

When a tall man strolled into the Safari Bar and peered around, Mack's hand went to the Colt .45 in his waistband, hoping he wouldn't have to use it.

The man smiled and waved to a woman sitting alone in the opposite corner. As he hurried to her Mack let out a sigh of relief.

Hilda lowered the phone from her ear and said, "My father will have the information we need on Marek Gullberg by the time we get there. Let's go."

Mack followed Hilda out the back door of the Safari Bar into the dimly lit alley. They weaved their way around small delivery vans, dumpsters and rows of bicycles until they reached a well-lit pedestrian walkway.

"Your wet clothes will attract unwanted attention so we stay off the roads with cars as much as possible," Hilda said. "It will only take us few minutes longer."

Ten minutes later, Hilda stopped in front of nondescript iron door. She slid the key in and said, "This takes us up to my father's office."

"I know," Mack said. "I went out this door earlier."

The passageway was a gradual climb up until reaching a narrow set of stairs. At the top of the stairs, Hilda knocked once on the door, paused five seconds than knocked twice.

The door slid open automatically. Peter sat at his desk with a small notebook computer open in front of him. He waved Mack and Hilda over then turned the computer toward them.

"Is this the man from Keller Bank you asked about?"

Mack nodded.

"His name is Marek Gullberg. He's been at Keller Bank his entire career."

Mack took a closer look at Gullberg's photo on the screen. "Where can I find him?"

"Where can *we* find him?" Hilda said.

Peter brought up a map on the screen. "He lives on *Chapfstrasse* in Zumikon, a town on the outskirts of Zürich. It's only about ten minutes from here."

Hilda looked at the map on the screen and said, "I know exactly where that is. We need a car." She looked at her father and grinned.

"Approach him with caution. There may be others interested in him." Peter handed Hilda the car keys. "Put on the Zürich plates and I will have the car registered to Keller Bank in case someone is keeping tabs on him and gets suspicious."

"I'll be back in few minutes," Hilda said. "I want to change clothes."

Mack waited until Hilda slipped out a side door before he sat in the chair across from Peter's desk.

"You have quite a daughter there," Mack said.

"I know," Peter answered proudly. "I nearly lost her and I'm not about to let that happen again." Peter explained how his family was abducted and held for ransom in exchange for his life. His voice was barely audible when he detailed how Hilda escaped. He nearly broke down when he described finding the bodies of his wife and son. When he finished, he sat up with a determined look on his face.

"Was that the reason you stopped working with Ray Gunn and disappeared?"

"No, but it was the final straw."

"If I may ask, what else drove your decision?"

Peter rubbed his thumbnail across his teeth as he thought about his answer or even if he would answer.

After a pensive pause, he said, "What started the ball rolling was an operation to expose and shut down a sex trafficking ring we believed was controlled by the Russians. Girls, mostly under the age of fifteen, were mysteriously disappearing from all over Eastern Europe, primarily Ukraine, Hungary and Slovakia. Many of these girls were found in high-end brothels in the US and Europe while others were sold into white slavery in the Middle East.

"I went undercover and maneuvered my way to the top echelon of the operation. After a year, I was able to get close to the people on the ground nabbing and selling the girls. A husband and wife team was running the operation from the Ukrainian city of Kharkiv, the country's second largest city. These were two sick, despicable people who abused many of these girls. The wife was the worst of the two. If a girl even looked like trouble, she beat the girl to within an inch of her life. It was the worst assignment of my life but too important to walk away from. To make a long story short, I was about to expose the entire operation when my cover was blown. One of my informants tipped me off that the couple was going to execute me. So, I made my way to their home on the edge of the city and waited for them. I knew their place and was able to slip inside without being noticed. The husband stumbled upon me, pulled his piece then hesitated. I didn't hesitate and blew off the top of his head. A couple seconds later, his wife came at me with a butcher's knife and I put one between her eyes." Peter stopped talking and stared off in the distance, his eyes blank.

After a minute, he sniffed and said, "There was young girl, a teenager, standing in the hall in a state of shock, staring at me. She was definitely old enough to identify me. My training kicked in and I instinctively raised my gun. I aimed at her head but couldn't pull the trigger. That's when I started to shake. The girl screamed and ran off. I heard a rush of footsteps so I boogied out of there. Less than a year later, my family was taken and you know the rest."

Mack felt the excruciating pain erupting from Peter's face. There was nothing he could think of to say.

The side door opened saving Mack.

Hilda walked in dressed in tight black pants, a long-sleeve black shirt and soft-soled black shoes. Her blonde hair was pulled back under a black baseball cap.

"Let's go make a withdrawal," she said.

Peter closed his computer and spun in his desk chair. "Before you go, Ray Gunn asked me to fill you in on what I know about the Ukrainian group running the sex trafficking ring. They go by the name *The Mogilschiiki*, or more simply *The Mogils*."

"Vlad already filled us in on *The Mogils*," Hilda replied.

"He doesn't know what I know. I walked among them. This despicable hornets nest goes deeper, much deeper. Human life doesn't mean shit to them."

$

# CHAPTER 19

Hilda walked around the large wooden desk and stood face to face with Peter. "You can fill us in on the *Mogils* when we get back from having our chat with the banker."

Mack sat in the chair in front of Peter's desk and gestured for Hilda to sit in the chair next to him. He said, "This is more important. Your dad will tell us what we need to know about the *Mogils*."

Peter waited for Hilda to sit before he sat down in his desk chair. "The *Mogils* live by the money rule. They care about one thing and one thing only, money. If someone gets in their way, their first instinct is to kill. They don't trust anybody they don't know. Hell, they barely trust each other. It took me over a year and a million dollars to form a loose partnership. I bought more girls from them than I care to admit. Luckily, we were able to get the families of those girls to America and reunite them.

"The *Mogils* promised me an unlimited supply of young girls but unfortunately I didn't have an unlimited supply of money. That being said, all transactions were in dollars and we knew the serial numbers on each and every note. We were able to trace the money to banks in Kiev and Moscow. The cash was then washed through pass-through companies owned by a private equity firm."

Mack interrupted, "Let me guess, Sunden Capital?"

Peter's eyes widened. "Yeah, how did you know?"

"Educated guess."

"What does this have to do with the *Mogils*?" Hilda asked. "There are tons of firms set up to launder money."

Mack grinned. "Sunden Capital is owned by J Otis Weil. He masquerades as a private equity investor but is really the banker to the Russian President, the Russian Mafia and to criminal groups like the *Mogils*."

Hilda crossed her arms, impatient to pay a visit with Marek Gullberg. "What's your point?"

Mack was about to reply when Peter raised his hand and said, "I got this."

Mack turned and faced Hilda to see her reaction.

Hilda didn't care to be studied by Mack as if she were the apprentice.

Peter realized what Mack was doing and waited for Hilda to turn her full attention back to him. He said, "Vlad doesn't know what I know. Sunden Capital not only launders the *Mogils*' illicit money, it finances their operations. This means the Russian President knows what the *Mogils* are up to and at best turns a blind eye to it. All he cares about is his cut, which is laundered by Sunden Capital. He needs the money to be untraceable."

Hilda dropped her hands to her lap and leaned forward. "I still don't know what this has to do with the missing intel money and the people who shot Siva and Vlad."

"I was giving you the long version," Peter answered. "Let me shorten it. The missing money from Keller Bank was to be used to sew unrest in Russia and bring down the Russian President as payback for Russia meddling in the elections in the

US, Britain and Israel. Somehow, the Russian President found out about the plan and the money. He ordered someone to steal the money and the *Mogils* were hired to kill anyone involved."

"This is where J Otis enters the picture," Mack said. "If we figure out his involvement and who he's working with here in Zürich, we find the money and who is after Siva and me."

"That's only part of the picture," Peter added. "The *Mogils* have to be found and... eliminated." Peter found it impossible to use the word *kill* in front of his daughter.

"You can say the word *kill,* dad. Because that's what I'll do when I find the people that shot Vlad and Siva and tried to kill me."

Peter grimaced.

Hilda thought it was because he didn't like her response then the real reason hit her. "These *Mogils* are the ones who killed mom and Stevie."

Uncomfortable where the conversation was headed, Mack rose from his chair and said, "Let's get rolling on this. We have a banker to visit."

Hilda stood and said, "Our car is in the underground garage of the building next door. Fortunately, we don't have to go outside to get into the garage."

The underground garage had low concrete ceiling. Mack instinctively ducked his head as they walked across the floor. In the corner was a plain gray Volkswagen Golf, a common car in Zürich.

Hilda opened the hatchback, removed two license plates and screwed them on the front and back.

As Hilda drove the car out of the garage, Mack asked, "Where exactly are we headed?"

"We're going to the town of Zumikon, not far outside the city. You might say it's Zürich's last suburb on this side of the lake."

Hilda waited for a city bus to pass then turned right onto *Forchstrasse*. "We take this road all the way into Zumikon and then go up the hill to Gullberg's apartment."

"I hope he's there," Mack said.

"He's there."

"How do you know?"

"When I changed clothes, I called Vlad and he arranged for someone he trusts to call Gullberg and verify he was there."

Five minutes later, Mack read the blue city sign:

ZUMIKON.

Hilda turned left at the first street, went straight through a roundabout, past a *Migros* grocery store and turned right. The road began a long, slow uphill climb.

A half-mile up the hill, Hilda said, "You see that pink building up on the right?"

"With the pointed roof?"

"Yes, Marek Gullberg lives on the top floor."

"How are we approaching this?"

"The building houses multiple apartments so that means it has a main entrance and a second, fire exit in back. We slip in the back and make our way up to his door. I'll knock and he'll let me in. You come in behind me."

"Sounds too easy."

"I'll take my hat off and let my hair down. Gullberg is a private banker so you can bet he's a player, or at least thinks he is. All I need is for him to open the door."

Hilda eased up on the gas pedal. "There's a car parked across the street with two people inside. I'll turn right past the apartment and park down the hill, out of sight."

Mack lowered his seat back and closed his eyes. He pretended to be asleep.

"You can sit up now," Hilda said. "In the car were two men, both wearing ties. My bet is they're here to keep an eye on Gullberg."

$

A block from the apartment, Hilda parked the car and looked at Mack. "I take the lead on this. Once we're inside, you can ask the questions but until then you do as I say. Do you have a problem with that?"

"I played baseball so I'm used to being told what to do."

A perplexed look washed over Hilda's face. "Excuse me?"

"In baseball if you don't do what the manager wants, you sit on the bench. I hated sitting on the bench."

Hilda readied her weapon. "Rule number one, stay behind me until we're inside. I don't want you in my sight line and have to shoot you. Rule number two, don't speak unless your life depends on it."

Mack nodded.

"Do you have your piece?"

Mack pulled out his Colt .45 and held it up.

"Good, but don't fire at anything or anyone near me." Hilda flicked her eyebrows up. "You may hit me instead."

"I don't plan on firing unless my life depends on it."

Hilda looked back up the hill at the peaked roof of Gullberg's apartment jutting above the neighboring house. "We cut between these two houses and come up to his apartment building from the backside. Keep your footfalls light and pray there are no dogs out."

Mack didn't reply. It wasn't life or death.

Hilda walked between the houses as if she was walking on the tips of the blades of grass.

Mack tried to copy her but his steps were heavy.

Hilda turned her head around and glared at him.

Mack grimaced and mouthed, "I'm trying." He lightened his step and before he knew it had copied Hilda's silent gait.

At the back corner of the apartment building, Hilda whispered, "Stay her until I get the back door open. Keep a watch on the street up there. I'll signal you when it's clear to move."

Mack pressed his back against the wall and steadily rotated his gaze to the street above, perusing the surroundings as he went.

A minute later he heard what sounded like a cricket's chirp. He leaned his head around the corner to see Hilda waving him over.

When Mack was inside, Hilda silently closed the door and squatted to a knee. Mack followed suit. The walls and the floor were thick gray concrete. To the right was a thick concrete door with a large vault latch.

Hilda followed Mack's eyes. With her voice barely audible, she said, "That's the bomb shelter. Every building in Switzerland is required to have a bomb shelter."

Mack nodded as if he understood why.

"As we go up, stay two steps behind me and listen for any noises behind you. Those steps over there will take us up to Gullberg's door. We stop and assess the situation a couple steps below."

Mack waited for Hilda to get a few feet in front of him then half crouched and followed, matching her pace.

Three steps from the front entrance, Hilda raised her clenched fist for Mack to stop. She stood stock-still, listening to the noises coming from the apartments above.

Satisfied everyone in the building was inside their apartment, she wiggled her fingers for Mack to follow her up the stairs.

On the top floor, Hilda handed her black hat to Mack and said, "Stay out of sight until Gullberg answers the door and I get one foot inside." She shook her head freeing her blonde hair.

Mack stepped out of sight keeping one eye on the stairs below. He quieted his mind and focused his attention on the sounds around him.

He heard Hilda knock firmly followed by the muted sound of footsteps growing closer. When the door opened, he heard a man say, "Can I help you?"

Mack peeked one eye around the corner to see Hilda stick her pistol under Gullberg's chin and say, "You and I need to talk."

Hilda pushed the door open and stepped inside, the pistol now jammed in Gullberg's chest. Fear engulfed Gullberg's eyes. He raised his arms and took a fearful step back.

Hilda spun Gullberg around and said, "Let's go inside and have a little chat. Don't do anything stupid."

Without saying a word, Mack followed Hilda

inside.

Gullberg's steps were hesitant and unsteady as he walked down the long hall into his apartment.

The first door on the right was a bedroom with an antique armoire against the far wall. A few steps further on the left was the door to the master bedroom. Mack peeked in to see a built-in closet with a row of dark suits hanging inside.

Walking into the living area, Hilda said, "Go sit on the sofa, Mr. Gullberg and keep your hands where I can see them."

Gullberg plopped down on the sofa and let out a loud sigh. He kept his eyes on Hilda's hand holding the pistol she was pointing at him.

Mack strolled around looking at the black and white pictures hanging on the wall. He stopped in front of a picture of Gullberg, Keller and a woman standing in front of Keller Bank.

Hilda waited until Mack joined her and said, "My friend here has a few questions for you. You will answer them truthfully and completely."

Gullberg looked over at Mack. Recognizing him, he said, "You are Siva Afari's accomplice."

"Accomplice infers I committed a crime. I suggest you choose another word. How about victim?"

Gullberg clenched his teeth, his jaw muscles tightened and he turned a shade of pink.

Mack was pleased by Gullberg's reaction. He was afraid and unable to hide it. "Mr. Gullberg, what we're going to discuss is the money, the hundred million, that went missing from Siva Afari's account."

"It wasn't her money," Gullberg replied, his voice quivering.

Mack walked up to Gullberg and leaned in close. "Siva Afari is in the hospital clinging to life after somebody shot her in cold blood. The only time you open your mouth is when you answer my questions. You understand?"

Gullberg nodded sheepishly.

"When Siva met with you at the bank, you informed her the money in her account was transferred out and the balance was zero. Walk me through what happened at that meeting."

Gullberg swallowed hard then cleared his throat. "After Ms. Afari came to the bank and did her business, I was asked to pull up the account and the transaction history for confirmation. You were right when you said the balance was zero. The transaction history indicated the transfer was initiated by Ms. Afari and all the security protocols were properly followed."

"Walk me through the security protocols."

Gullberg squirmed in his seat then sat up. "The first protocol is the electronic hand scan. Before entering the bank, clients must place their right hand on an electronic scanner. If it's a match, the client is led to one of our client transaction rooms. There, the client enters a nine-digit passcode that allows access to the private rooms. No personal items are allowed in the private rooms. Once inside, the client has use of a secure computer where a thumb print and voice recognition are required. When the computer is activated, the client then inputs a personal password and the account number. That gives the client access to their account at the bank. After the client is finished, the banker walks the client out of the bank."

"Are you with the client the entire time they are in the bank?"

"All bankers must be with the client up to the time the computer is activated. Before the client sits at the computer, the banker is required to leave the room."

"Were you with Ms. Afari up until the time you were required to leave the room?"

Gullberg glanced over at the gun in Hilda's hand. "Can she stop pointing that at me?"

"Not until we're done. Now answer my question."

"I never saw Ms. Afari until she was escorted to my office after her business was completed," Gullberg answered as his hands trembled.

"Who brought her to your office?"

"One of the bank's security officers."

"Is that normal protocol?"

Gullberg shook his head.

"Who at Keller Bank walked Ms. Afari through the security protocols?"

"Mercedes Geissel."

"If you are Ms. Afari's banker, why didn't you walk her through security? She was your client."

Sweat began for form on Gullberg's forehead. "Before Mercy was promoted to head of client services, she handled all of the bank's Double D accounts." His words were now coming out in rapid fire. "She was Ms. Afari's banker for this account but we were in the process of transferring the account to me. That was before I gave my one month notice to resign from the bank."

"Double D account? What is that?"

"That stands for *Distinctive and Discreet.* That's the designation for accounts belonging to intelligence services. We have special rules and provisions for those accounts. Do you want me to tell you what those are?"

"No need. If you are resigning from the bank, why did you meet with Ms. Afari?"

"Mercy Geissel asked me to. While Ms. Afari was in the private client room, Mercy brought me Ms. Afari's personal items, her handbag and phone. That's when she informed me a security officer was escorting Ms. Afari to my office and ordered me to walk her out."

Mack rolled his eyes. "Why did she ask you to walk her out?"

"Ms. Afari was being belligerent and unreasonable. Mercy was certain Ms. Afari transferred the money and then tried to run a scam on the bank. It's not the first time some hack tried to bilk us out of money."

"Hack?" Mack took a deep, calming breath to keep from clobbering Gullberg with both fists.

"Do you have cameras inside the bank?" Hilda asked while Mack was calming down.

"No, not inside the bank. Our clients require the strictest secrecy and don't want cameras anywhere near the client rooms. To nearly everyone at the bank, our clients are just numbers and our clients prefer it that way. There are security cameras outside the bank but none are allowed where clients go once they're inside, that's bank policy."

Mack recalled Gullberg taking pictures of him and Siva with his phone. He clenched his fists and asked, "Then why did you take my picture outside the bank? I thought cameras were against bank policy."

Gullberg blinked repeatedly and said, "I was ordered to by Mercy. It was a precaution in case Ms. Afari took legal action."

Mack started to walk to the door then stopped, turned around and said, "Here's what you're going to do. Tomorrow, you'll go into the bank and get me the security logs with accompanying time stamps for each step Ms. Afari went through as well as the wire transfer information."

Gullberg wiped the sweat from his forehead and said, "I can't do that."

"That's the wrong answer."

"It's the only answer I can give. I was walked out of the bank today. Before I left, my bank ID was taken and my security codes and system access were deleted from the bank's system. Even if I wanted to help you, there's no way I can."

That was not what Mack wanted to hear. "Who can get that information for me?"

"You have to talk to Lee Khandelwal, he's the Chief Technology Officer and head of bank security."

"What time does he normally get into his office?"

"He's usually in by nine, but tomorrow's Saturday. Lee never works weekends."

"Where does he live?"

"In Herrliberg, which is down the lake from here."

"I know Herrliberg well," Hilda said. "I can get his address."

"I have one more question for you... for now."

Gullberg moved to stand and Mack pushed him back down in his seat.

"Why did you resign from Keller Bank?"

"I took a better job at a new private bank in town. I will be head of client services there." Gullberg tried to grin proudly.

"Give me the name of your new bank in case I have more questions for you."

"JOW Private Bank. The charter was just approved by the banking authorities and we open for business next week. I have our new marketing brochure and the bank's charter on the table over there." Gullberg pointed to the dining table to his right.

Hilda flicked her pistol at the table and said, "Lead the way, Mr. Gullberg."

Gullberg trudged over to the table and handed the marketing brochure to Mack. "We used this to raise the necessary capital."

Mack flipped open the brochure and paged through it. He froze when he came to the headshots of the Board of Directors. He whispered, "Son of a Bitch." He held the page up for Hilda to see.

It took a second for Hilda eyes to reach the last head shot at the bottom of the page. She shook violently as her face burned deep red. Tears rolled down her cheeks. "That's the bastard who raped me."

Mack threw the brochure back on the table, turned and walked away. He stopped in front of the picture of Gullberg with Keller and a woman in front of the bank. "Mr. Gullberg, who's the woman in this picture with you and Beat Keller?"

Gullberg hesitated then said, "Why is that important?"

Hilda stuck her pistol under Gullberg's chin. "Answer his question."

"That's Mercedes Geissel."

"She handles all intel accounts, right?"

Gullberg nodded meekly. "Yes, but she was recently promoted to run the day-to-day operations."

Hearing Gullberg's disappointed and defeated tone, Mack asked, "Did you want that job? Or, should I say, did you expect to get that job?"

Gullberg didn't answer. He merely shrugged.

Hilda pushed her pistol harder against Gullberg chin. "If you tell anyone about our little chat, I will come back, stick my gun where it is now and pull the trigger."

From the sweat pouring down Gullberg's forehead, she knew he'd keep his mouth shut. On her way out she snatched the brochure off the table.

$

# CHAPTER 20

Back inside the car, Hilda stared blankly out the windshield. She wiped the tears running down her cheeks and turned to face Mack. Seeing J Otis' face, even if it was just a picture in brochure, had thrown her for a loop. She dreamed of finding the bastard but never thought that day would come. She sniffed, readying herself for the fight to come.

"Tell me what you know about J Otis Weil," she demanded.

"I'll tell you everything on the drive over."

"On the drive over where?"

"To the hospital to check on Siva."

"It's almost midnight. Even if Siva is out of surgery and has regained consciousness, she'll be asleep. You can wait until morning. You should wait, she needs rest."

Mack pondered Hilda's logic as she started the car and shifted into gear.

He said, "If you want to learn what I know about J Otis Weil, drive me to the hospital."

When Hilda didn't reply, Mack said, "You can check on Vlad while we're there."

The car rolled down the darkened street with its headlights off. When they reached the first street light, Hilda turned on the headlights and said, "Fine, but I think it's a bad idea. We should be paying a visit to Khandelwal. According to Gullberg, Khandelwal is the key to finding who took the money and shot Siva and Vlad."

"We can do that first thing in the morning. It will still give us the element of surprise. He won't be expecting anyone on a Saturday morning."

They drove in silence until they were on the main road back into Zürich.

Hilda eased up on the gas pedal. "Now that we're on our way to the hospital tell me about J Otis Weil."

Mack scratched his chin. Where did he start with someone like J Otis?

"Before I tell you what I know about him, I will give you my impression of him as a human being, and I use that term loosely."

"He's a rapist and a pedophile," Hilda said, "that tells me everything I need to know about him as a human being."

"It's not as simple as that."

"It is for me."

"You're not wrong but when you confront him, it's best you know everything about him."

"Just give me what I need to know to kill him."

"Fine but don't interrupt me. When I finish, you can ask your questions, agreed?"

"If you say so."

Mack concentrated on the headlights of the car coming at them in the on-coming lane as he weighed his words. When the car zipped past he checked the receding red lights in the side mirror then said, "J Otis is like the smart-ass little kid who hides behind his friends as he smarts off to the bigger kids then runs away as fast as possible, laughing as he goes. By that, I mean he's a coward." Mack thought the word coward gave the wrong impression. "J Otis is a coward but a dangerous coward. I tell you this because he makes it difficult for anyone to get close to him. If you do get close, you will have one chance, one shot to get him."

"That's all I need," Hilda replied matter-of-factly.

The chilling tone of Hilda's voice spooked Mack. "I can't even begin to understand what you went through but don't underestimate J Otis, he's an evil little man and a sneaky little shit. Those types are the most dangerous."

"Point taken."

"J Otis considers himself a private equity investor. In reality, he's the banker to criminal undergrounds around the world. His specialty is human trafficking, specifically young girls to work in the sex trade. He is also the private banker to the Russian President and his cronies."

"Those are some powerful friends."

"He uses them for his protection and they use him for his money laundering expertise so I wouldn't call them friends, per se. As long as J Otis serves their purpose, he's allowed to keep breathing. If he ever crosses them, you'll never find his bullet-riddled body. It'll be at the bottom of Lake Baikal in Siberia. That being said, J Otis lives in Moscow and when he travels outside Russia, he uses one of his many aliases."

"Passing himself off as Russian?" Hilda asked.

"No, he can't speak a word of Russian. He's lived there for over fifteen years and still can't speak a word of Russian. He uses forged American or Canadian passports the Russian government provides." Mack watched a train pass along the side of the road, heading in the opposite direction, away from the city.

"From the best of my knowledge, J Otis only leaves the protection of Moscow when there will be a transfer of money to his account. He is a mastermind of skirting international wire transfer regulations and he needs to be at the wire source to make certain there is no money trail. That being said, the most important thing to remember is he lives by the creed, 'it's only illegal if you get caught.' He applies that to everything in his life."

"He kept saying he was giving me a thrill every time he raped me," Hilda said with a shutter.

"He's a sociopath, maybe even a psychopath."

"What's his weakness? You must know that."

"Besides his fragile ego, he has an unhealthy infatuation with young teenage girls. Thirteen or fourteen year-olds are his preference. I have to believe that's why he aggressively finances the sex trafficking networks. He considers the young girls a fringe benefit. That's pretty much what you need to know about J Otis Weil."

Hilda drove in silence until they reached the city limits. "I can pass myself off as a teenager and use that to my advantage, lure him in and then do what needs to be done."

Mack was disturbed by Hilda's response. "Don't play games with him. He may remember you. Hit him head-on before he knows what's happening. If you don't, he'll either have one of his goons go at you or he'll turn and hightail out... runaway like a little girl... Sorry, bad choice of words. But, remember this, if he gets away you'll have a target on your head for the rest of your life or until J Otis is dead."

Hilda didn't reply. She calmly grinned.

$

# CHAPTER 21

The final two miles of the drive to the hospital was a white-knuckle ride for Mack. Hilda paid no attention to Zürich traffic laws and sped past three speed camera. All three flashed brightly.

"What the-" Mack started to say.

Hilda cut him off. "This car won't be registered to anyone in Switzerland by tomorrow and I'll go online and erase the pictures."

Mack stared out the window for the remainder of the drive through the city, his right hand gripping the door handle.

Walking up the steps to the hospital, Mack had his composure back and said, "It's after visiting hours so we have to be either a parent or a spouse to get in. I will go in first as Siva's husband. Wait a couple minutes and come in as Vlad's wife. I'll wait for you outside Siva's room."

Hilda frowned, "We should just walk in like we own the place but if that makes it easier, fine."

Mack strolled up to the reception desk and asked to see his wife who was rushed into the emergency room earlier in the evening. The receptionist looked skeptically at Mack then at her computer screen. She wrote down Mack's full name then gave him Siva's room number and pointed down the hall.

Hilda waited for Mack to disappear down the hall. She approached the receptionist and asked to see her husband who was rushed to the emergency room. The receptionist studied the screen, wrote down Hilda's name and said Vlad was being treated in the emergency room. She pointed in the opposite direction from where Mack went.

Hilda started down the same hall as Mack when the receptionist said, "Excuse me, the emergency room is down the other hall." She pointed emphatically to her left.

"I'm sorry, I am just so flustered because my husband is in the hospital." Hilda smiled apologetically. "This way, you said."

The receptionist nodded and kept her eyes on Hilda.

While Mack stood outside the door to Siva's room waiting for Hilda, a young doctor strolled by and walked into Siva's room. Mack peeked inside as the doctor entered. He saw Siva lying in the bed with tubes and wires attached to various parts of her body. Sitting at the foot of the bed was Vlad who greeted the doctor with a sorrowful smile.

Five minutes later, the doctor emerged from the room looking solemn.

"Excuse me doctor," Mack said. "Do you speak English?"

"Of course," the doctor replied. "How can I help you?"

"Siva Afari is my fiancé and I just learned about her being shot. What can you tell me about her condition?" Mack's eyes teared up as he spoke.

The doctor looked Mack up and down then focused on his eyes. "Siva was shot through the hip by a high-caliber weapon. The bullet went through, which is good, but the area the bullet traveled through holds a number of critical organs. She's incurred significant damage to a number of those organs." The doctor grimaced as he said this and let his words sink in. When Mack nodded, he continued, "We were able to stop the bleeding, which is critical to her survival. But, she will require more surgery to repair the damage."

"Are you saying she'll be fine?"

The doctor put his hand on Mack's shoulder and held his gaze. "It is too soon to know. There is the chance the organs are too damaged to repair or she develops an infection. If either of those happen, her chances of survival are severely diminished. We are doing everything we can. I'm sorry I don't have better news for you."

"What are her chances?"

"We won't know until we see the damage to her organs."

"What can I do?"

"If you're a religious man, pray."

As the doctor strolled away, a tear rolled down Mack's cheek. Across the hall was an empty visitor's lounge. Mack meandered over, flicked on the lights and sat on the sofa by the door.

He wiped the tear from his cheek then dropped his head and rubbed his eyes. Looking up, he saw Hilda standing in the doorway.

"What's wrong? Is Siva okay?"

"She's not out of the woods yet. She needs more surgery before the doctors know anything."

Hilda took Mack by the arm and led him to Siva's door. "Vlad was not in the emergency room. The nurse said he left after they treated his leg but before his paperwork was completed. They didn't know where he went."

"He's in with Siva."

Hilda pushed open the door to Siva's room. She raised her finger over her shoulder and wiggled it for Mack to follow.

Inside, Vlad put his finger to his lips then pointed out to the hall. He strolled into the visitor's lounge across the hall, rearranged the chairs so three faced Siva's door and gestured for Mack and Hilda to sit.

"Fill me in," Vlad said. "You never tell what happen with Keller visit."

Mack walked him through his encounter with Keller and the subsequent attack. He described the attackers as amateur commandos who didn't secure the target before attacking.

"Sounds like how the *Mogils* operate," Vlad said as if from experience.

"It sounded like they were speaking Russian or a dialect of Russian."

"The *Mogils* speak Russian because they want Ukraine to belong to Russia," Vlad replied. "How *Mogils* know you were at Keller house?"

"Good question," Mack said. "It was obvious Keller wasn't expecting them. If he were involved, they would have been there waiting for me when I arrived."

"Who tipped the *Mogils* off?" Hilda asked.

Mack closed his eyes as he contemplated the possible suspects. He opened his eyes to see Vlad with his arm around Hilda's shoulders. "It has to either be someone close to Keller like his bodyguard, someone at Keller Bank or, and this one scares me, someone betraying Ray Gunn."

"Is someone in bank," Vlad said. "I am sure."

Hilda said, "We visited Gullberg, who worked for Keller."

Mack gave a detailed description of their encounter with Gullberg. At the end, he said, "I don't think Gullberg is involved but that's only my gut speaking."

"Either he's involved and is good at playing dumb or may be involved and doesn't know it," Hilda said. "His story is impossible to verify until we pay a visit to Khandelwal."

"Who is Khandelwal?" Vlad asked.

"He's the bank's Chief Technology Officer and head of security," Mack answered. "If anyone knows what happened to the money and who took it, it'll be him."

"What you do if Khandelwal involved?" Vlad looked at Mack as he asked the question. When Mack hesitated to answer, he glanced over at Hilda.

"Everyone has a breaking point," Hilda said. "And he knows everything going on at the bank."

"Let's not jump that far ahead just yet. We have to consider the possible betrayal of Ray Gunn by someone." Mack raised his pointer finger and said, "We have Herr Schmidt who drove me to the meeting with Keller." He raised his middle finger. "There's also the CIA operative living in Liechtenstein. He funded the account on behalf of the intel agencies."

"Highly improbable," Hilda said. "They didn't know you were meeting Keller at his house until you went there. We can't eliminate them but we should put them at the bottom of the list. It has to be Gullberg or Khandelwal. I think we should go see Khandelwal now, while he's sleeping."

"That will scare hell out of him," Vlad added.

"Let's think this through," Mack said. "Someone has known our every move so far. When you left the Safari Bar for the secret apartment, did you notice anyone following you?"

Hilda thought for a second then shook her head. "We should also consider that Keller was the target and not you, Billy."

"Too much of a coincidence," Billy replied. The attack at the apartment and the raid at Keller's house happened too close together. Someone knows our every move."

Vlad stared off in the distance as he re-ran the walk from the Safari Bar to the apartment. He shook his head, certain they weren't followed. Then, as if a light went on in his head, he said, "I went through Siva's handbag and found this sitting at the bottom." He held up a thin, smooth silver object that resembled a dime. "I thought it was lucky coin or something. Now I think, why Siva have American money in purse?" He placed it on the tile floor and smashed it with the heel of his boot. The object cracked open to reveal tiny electronics.

"Damn it," Mack said, "that's a tracking device."

Outside in the hall, a man in a white doctor's coat, a stethoscope around his neck and a clipboard in the right hand strolled up to Siva's door. He glanced down the hall, knocked softly then gently pushed open the door.

"That's strange," Mack said. "That doctor was wearing only one rubber glove."

"Which hand?" Vlad asked.

"His left hand."

"Son of Bitch." Vlad jumped out of this chair, sprinted across the hall and burst into Siva's room.

$

# CHAPTER 22

Mack and Hilda jumped from their chairs and chased after Vlad. Crossing the hall, they heard two stifled gunshots. Mack burst through the door to see Vlad standing over the man in the white smock. Vlad had shot him in his right shoulder and right thigh.

Vlad's stood over the man digging his heel into the man's bloody thigh as he searched him for weapons. He pulled a knife from the man's back pocket then ripped off the rubber glove from his left hand to reveal a tattoo of two snakes wrapped around a stick.

"He is *Mogil*."

Mack saw a syringe sticking out of Siva's arm. He rushed over and carefully removed the needle. He looked over at Hilda. "Go get help, a doctor or a nurse. Hurry."

Mack ripped off his belt, wrapped it around Siva's bicep, pulled it tight and held it hoping to stop whatever was shot into Siva's arm from reaching her head and her heart.

Vlad smacked the *Mogil* in the temple with butt of his pistol, knocking him out. He grabbed him by his hair and dragged him out of the room and into the visitor's lounge.

A doctor running to Siva's room saw the injured *Mogil* being dragged into the visitor's lounge and turned to go help him.

Hilda grabbed the doctor by the arm and yelled, "In here first doctor." She dragged the doctor into Siva's room.

The doctor reluctantly followed. Seeing the color of Siva's face alarmed him and he hurried to her bed. He put his hand on her forehead and studied her face. Her skin was clammy and cool. She was barely breathing and there was a gurgle in her throat. Her lips had begun turning blue.

A nurse appeared at the door and stopped in her

tracks when the doctor said, "It's a heroin overdose. Bring me naloxone right away."

Mack and Hilda felt helpless staring at Siva motionless in her bed.

Fifteen seconds later, the nurse reappeared at the door with an automatic injector in her hand. She held it up as she ran over to Siva and handed the injector across the bed.

The doctor removed Mack's belt and dropped it on the floor. He jammed the injector into Siva's bicep until he heard the click then held her wrist to take her pulse. The nurse put her hand a half-inch from Siva's mouth to gauge the strength of her breathing.

An eerie silence penetrated the room. Mack felt his heart beating hard against his chest. He didn't take his eyes off Siva as he recited a silent prayer he'd learned in grade school.

Three minutes later, the doctor let out a sigh and looked up. "Her pulse is stronger but not back to normal. Given her condition, someone will be at her bedside for the next twenty-four hours closely monitoring her."

"Her breathing is stronger," the nurse added.

"Whoever wrapped the belt around her arm saved her life," the doctor said.

Mack and Hilda grinned at the same time but didn't say a word.

"You two need to leave her to rest." The doctor turned to the nurse. "Stay with her until I can get someone to relieve you."

The doctor walked out and headed toward the visitor's lounge.

Hilda caught up to him in the hall and stopped him. "You can treat that guy when we're done talking to him."

The doctor opened his mouth to object. Mack stepped in front of the doctor and said, "That man in there just tried to kill Siva. Once we get what we need from him, we'll drag him down to the emergency room."

The look in Mack's eyes frightened the doctor and he involuntarily took a step back.

"Don't worry, we're not going to kill him. Once we get the information we need, he can get treatment."

"Someone shot that man," the doctor replied, his voice pleading.

Vlad heard the doctor's reply and walked out of the visitor's lounge. "That man pulled pistol on me when I try and stop him. When we finish you call police but you only call to arrest man who try to kill Siva, understood?"

The doctor nodded submissively and backed away. A few feet later, he spun around and walked away as fast as humanly possible without breaking into a full sprint.

"We better hurry," Mack said. "As soon as he gets back to his office, he's calling the cops."

Vlad walked over the man lying flat on the floor. He slapped him hard across the cheek and in Russian said, "Wake up."

The man stirred then opened his eyes and hesitantly sat up.

Vlad took the man's left hand and placed it palm down on the tile floor. He pressed the heel of his boot on top the man's hand.

Hilda grabbed the man's right hand and lifted it over his head.

Mack closed the door to the visitor's lounge.

The man came to, twisted his shoulder and screamed in pain from the bullet wound. When he moved, the pain became excruciating.

In Russian, Vlad asked, "Who sent you?"

The man shook his head. He wasn't about to

answer.

Vlad lifted his uninjured leg and slammed the heel of his boot down on the *Mogil's* hand. The sound of bones shattering sent a shiver through Mack.

Vlad looked over at Hilda. She twisted the man's arm, nearly dislocating his injured shoulder.

The man bit his tongue to stifle his scream.

Vlad leaned down, his nose an inch from the *Mogil's* nose. "This is the last time I ask. Who sent you?"

Hilda gave another twist for emphasis.

The *Mogil* screamed again. When Hilda eased the twist, the man said in English, "The man who pay us is Mr. Weil. He and banker friend pay me to kill woman. They not say why."

"Is the banker friend a bald man named Marek Gullberg?" Mack asked.

The *Mogil* looked strangely at Mack and said, "Is not man, is woman."

$

# CHAPTER 23

Vlad took his pistol from his waistband and slammed the butt into the *Mogil's* temple, much harder this time. His body shook violently. Vlad released his grip and the man dropped to the floor with a thud.

"We go see this Khandelwal now." Vlad said.

Mack looked over at Hilda to read her reaction. The look on her face was stoic. "What do you think?" he asked.

"After what happened to Siva, we don't have much time. I agree with Vlad but first we need to get

Siva moved to a different room on a different floor and get her registered under a different name. The *Mogils* know what room she's in and will send in a real pro next time."

"I'll go take care of it," Mack said. "You both get the car and meet me out front." He turned and marched to the nurse's station. On the way, he called Ray Gunn to give him an update and arrange for his contacts to run interference with the doctor and Swiss authorities.

It took Mack five minutes to confirm Siva was being moved to an undisclosed room. On his way out of the hospital, he stopped an orderly to tell him he saw a man bleeding in the visitor's lounge.

At the reception desk, Mack nodded and said a quiet thank you to the receptionist as he walked past.

Standing outside the main entrance were two men and a woman. All three were staring at him as he approached the door.

As soon as Mack stepped outside, the taller of the two men stepped forward. He carried a full head of hair and trimmed beard. "Are you William McMillan?"

"That's him," the woman said loudly and pointed at him like he was guilty. "He goes by Billy Mack."

The woman was five-feet four inches tall with brown hair and dark brown eyes. She wore a navy blazer, blue blouse and gray slacks.

"Call me Billy," Mack said and glanced over at the shorter man who'd moved off to the side. He had a thin face, a shaved head and his right hand was inside his sport coat. Mack knew what the man's hand was gripping inside his coat. "Is there something I can do for you?"

"We'd like you to come with us," the taller man said.

"I'm busy."

"We have a few questions for you and this is not the appropriate place to conduct our business."

"I'm going to need more than that." Mack looked at his watch as if time was of the essence.

The taller man grinned as if willing to play Mack's game. "We're interested in getting back our money."

"You're barking up the wrong tree. Siva and I had nothing to do with the money going missing." Mack started to walk away.

The shorter man took a step toward Mack and opened his sport coat to reveal his shoulder holster. "We're done asking."

Mack saw Hilda and Vlad sitting in the car on the street near the entrance to the circular driveway. The lights were off but the motor was running. He averted his eyes and gestured with his hands as if he were opening a book. He hoped she understood he meant for her to go to the bookstore.

Hilda put the car in gear and drove away with the car lights off.

Mack looked up and said, "Before I agree, I want to know who you are and why you're involved."

"Get in the car," the shorter man ordered and pointed to a dark Range Rover parked in a handicap spot just past the hospital entrance.

"Billy... may I call you Billy?" the taller man asked.

"Only if I know your name."

"It's Mickey, Mickey Giuliani." Giuliani stuck out his hand.

Mack reluctantly took his hand and shook it.

"Are you Billy Mack, the former baseball player?"

"That would be me."

"I saw you play a number of times in New York when the White Sox came to town. You were quite the ballplayer," Giuliani said still gripping Mack's hand. "Now get in the car."

On the way to the car, Giuliani said, "My colleagues are Israel Joe Paletz and Mercedes Geissel."

"Do you work together?"

"No," Giuliani answered as he opened the back door of the Range Rover and stood aside.

Mack suddenly recognized Mercedes Geissel from the picture in Gullberg's apartment. Was she the agent imbedded inside Keller bank that Peter mentioned?

The Range Rover drove out of the hospital's main entrance just as two police cruisers drove up to the front door. Mack instinctively slid down in his seat and turned his head away. Four cops jumped out from their cruisers, left their doors open and sprinted into the hospital.

Once the hospital was out of sight, Mack sat up. He read the street signs and memorized landmarks as they drove. They cruised through central Zürich, over the Sihl River and into a warehouse district. Below an overpass, Paletz turned the car down a dark side street, made a short right and pushed a button on the car's sun visor. The garage door in front of them rolled up.

Paletz eased the car to a stop in front of glass-walled office. "Follow us," he said to Mack.

Inside the office, Giuliani flicked on the lights and pointed to a room off to the right. "Go in there."

The room was long and narrow. A wooden table stood in the middle of the room. There were no chairs to be found anywhere in the room.

Mack leaned against the table and waited for Giuliani and Paletz to enter followed by the Geissel. They stood in a semi-circle in front of Mack.

Mack asked, "You three are interested in the money stolen from Siva's account, right?"

Geissel got in Mack's face. "You and Ms. Afari stole the money from the bank."

Mack laughed.

Geissel's face grew flush. "Our system shows that Ms. Afari went through the security procedures and transferred the money. After which, she met you. That equals one hundred million missing. Do the math."

Giuliani pulled Geissel away by the shoulder and said, "This is not a game, Billy."

Mack stayed silent. He wasn't about to respond. Nothing he said would matter.

Geissel jerked her shoulder away from Giuliani's grip. "We have the evidence that you and Afari worked with Marek Gullberg and Lee Khandelwal to transfer the money to a bank in Miami and into accounts, we know were established by you and Afari. Khandelwal went into the system with Gullberg's passwords, transferred the money then erased the transactions. He then overrode the system to reflect the transfers as going through the proper security procedures. I plan to give that evidence to the Swiss banking regulators to start criminal proceedings."

"Do what you gotta do," Mack said.

"I'm going to the bank to collect the evidence," Geissel said. She pointed first at Paletz then at Giuliani. "You keep him here until you hear from me." She strolled out the room and disappeared into the dark warehouse.

Giuliani and Paletz strolled out the room behind Geissel and stood just outside the door, conversing quietly.

Mack pushed himself up and sat on the table.

Giuliani walked back in the room while Paletz ambled over to the Range Rover with his phone stuck in his ear.

"What are you doing now, Billy?"

"Talking to you."

"Funny, I mean career-wise."

"I work with Baxter, Israel and Gunn. You may know it as BIG. I am the firm's troubleshooter. My job is to fix problems with the firm's investments."

"Gunn, as in Ray Gunn?" Giuliani asked.

"That'd be him."

Giuliani sat on the table a few feet from Mack. "Do you know what Gunn did before he founded BIG?"

Mack decided to be coy with his answer. "I have a vague idea but never probed."

"Gunn is a legend, a black ops legend. His operations are still taught at the Farm, to this day." Guiliani blushed realizing he'd given away too much information. "I guess you know what I do."

"You're an agent with the CIA."

"Technically I'm a NOC. Do you know what that is?"

"You're a spy who gets paid better."

Giuliani smiled broadly. "Never thought of it that way."

Paletz strolled back into the room with a worried

look on his face. "We got a problem."

"We need Dmitri, don't we?" Giuliani said.

"He's on his way."

$

# CHAPTER 24

"Who is Dmitri and why is he joining us?" Mack asked as he jumped off the table and stood.

Giuliani and Paletz looked at each other deciding who would answer.

Giuliani slid down off the table. "He's a technology consultant and an expert at navigating the dark web. That's why we brought him in."

"You mean he's a hacker."

Neither Guiliani nor Paletz answered.

"Does he work for you?" Mack directed the question at Giuliani.

"He's a freelancer and one of the most dangerous men not carrying a gun. He can ruin your life with a few key strokes on his computer."

"You trust him?"

"He's paid very well."

"What happens if someone pays him better?"

Giuliani grinned like that would never happen. "He was trained by Mossad's Unit 8200, the best of the best coders and hackers in the world. If he betrayed the Mossad, it would be the last thing he ever did and he knows it."

Paletz phone buzzed and he checked the screen. "Dmitri is outside. I'll go let him in."

Mack watched Paletz stroll away then looked over at Giuliani. "You said Dmitri is an expert in the dark web? I can understand bringing a hacker in but what does this dark web have to do with the missing money?"

"I'll let Dmitri explain it."

Paletz and Dmitri walked into the room. Dmitri was short and rail thin. His hair was light brown, parted down the middle and hung to his shoulders. He wore a green t-shirt and faded jeans. A strap attached to an old canvass postal bag was draped over his right shoulder.

Mack guessed the canvass bag weighed more than Dmitri.

Without acknowledging anyone in the room, Dmitri set the bag on the table and removed a laptop. He opened it and began typing.

The flat screen hanging on the wall came to life. A picture of Keller Bank came into focus.

"I will walk you through the money trail first. You can ask questions when I'm finished." Dmitri spoke with a British accent.

Mack pointed at Paletz and said, "You said we had a problem?"

"Dmitri," Paletz said, "do your magic."

Dmitri tapped a key on the keyboard and a slide show started.

"The money was transferred out of the Afari account at Keller Bank in two installments. The first was for $40 million to RD Bank in Bad Vöslau, Austria then sent on to Southern Bank in Miami. The remaining $60 million was wired directly to the same bank in Miami."

A picture of Southern Bank's glass and steel headquarters building slid across the screen.

"Southern Bank initiated a transfer of the full hundred million to Kharkiv Privat Bank in the Ukraine and into the account belonging to JOW East European Holdings, a subsidiary of JOW Panama. The address of JOW East European is a law firm based in Moscow. As a result, the transfer has been held up by the US Treasury while they verify the transfer does not violate the sanctions imposed on Russia."

Dmitri looked around to indicate he was finished.

"Does that mean the money is sitting in Miami?" Mack asked.

"Technically yes but it is merely an accounting entry."

"How long will it take for the Treasury Department to make their determination?"

"I will get to that in a minute."

"Let's take a step back," Giuliani said. "Were you able to get into Keller Bank's system to see who initiated the transaction?"

Dmitri nodded as he tapped the keyboard. A flow chart appeared on the screen.

"The system shows that Siva Afari, the account holder, followed the proper security procedures and initiated the transaction." Dmitri paused and held up his finger before Mack could interrupt.

"The system was overridden by someone."

"How can you know that?" Mack asked.

This time Dmitri raised both hands up gesturing for Mack to be patient. "Siva Afari was sitting in the reception area when the funds were transferred. I found a discrepancy at the time of the transfer. International wire transfers are executed through the SWIFT System. The SWIFT System recorded the transfer ten minutes before Keller Bank's system shows the transaction as recorded. If you compare the time on the SWIFT System with the bank's internal system, the computer timed to that transfer is the computer belonging to a banker named Marek Gullberg." Dmitri tapped the keyboard again. A black and white picture of Gullberg standing outside the bank smoking a cigarette popped on the screen. "What is interesting is that Gullberg was not in his office at that time. He was outside having a smoke. Bad, bad habit."

"What about Khandelwal? He has the ability to control the system and make any and all changes." Mack said.

"The time line doesn't fit that scenario," Dmitri

said. "Khandelwal had just returned from the Ukraine. His flight landed less than thirty minutes before the transfer was recorded by SWIFT."

"Can you be sure your information is accurate? I mean, Keller Bank supposedly has the most secure system in the world."

Dmitri let out a soft chuckle. "I've done work for the bank and have all their security codes and access points. All my information is spot-on accurate."

"Then that rules out Khandelwal," Giuliani said.

Paletz walked over to the screen and studied the flow chart. "Not if he went rogue and partnered with someone." Paletz pointed at the flow chart. "Khandelwal's as good as they get in cyber security. That means he knows all the tricks. If he did go rogue, we have a problem."

$

# CHAPTER 25

Mack, Giuliani and Dmitri gathered around the screen as Paletz traced his finger across the flow chart on the screen. "If Khandelwal is involved, my guess is he and Keller conspired to steal the money."

"Wrong again, Israel Joe," a voice coming from the doorway said. "I bet the missing hundred million bucks Keller is not involved. He doesn't have the stones. Besides, his bank makes too much money for him to do something that stupid. You add the fact that he was just attacked at his house and you can eliminate him from consideration."

All four heads staring at the screen turned to the left as if they were synchronized swimmers.

Peter stood in the doorway wearing a loose-fitting tweed sport coat. His gray hair was pulled back into a ponytail.

Mack smiled as he walked over and shook Peter's hand. He turned back around to see Giuliani, Paletz and Dmitri staring at Peter with their eyes wide and their mouths agape as if they'd seen a ghost.

Peter stepped into the room and said, "The prodigal son returns."

Giuliani took a tentative step toward Peter, stopped, shook his head in disbelief then hurried to Peter.

"Tom Garrahan, you're supposed to be dead." He hugged Peter then took a step back.

Paletz and Dmitri strolled over slowly, disbelief washed across their faces.

"What's going on, Peter?" Mack asked.

"My real name is Tom Garrahan. But until my situation is resolved, I'm still Peter."

Mack walked over to the door, peeked out then walked back inside. "Are Hilda and Vlad with you?"

"No, they're back at the bookstore. I had to use

every persuasive trick in the book to get Hilda to stay there. She was hell-bent on finding J Otis Weil and killing him."

Dmitri grabbed Peter's hand and shook it vigorously. He released his grip and said, "I was so sorry when I heard about your wife and son."

Peter dropped his eyes to the floor. "Thank you."

Giuliani and Paletz both gave Peter their condolences.

Peter said, "You're probably wondering why I'm here."

"The *Mogilschiiki*," Dmitri answered. He walked over to his computer and frantically typed on the keyboard. A list of websites came on the screen.

"These websites are on the dark web."

"What the hell is this dark web I hear so much about?" Mack asked.

"It's where someone goes in order to find things that are illegal."

"Why don't governments shut them down?"

"Easier said then done. These websites look normal but when you move the cursor over a picture or an icon, the address or a link for the illegal site pops up. Most users are discreetly directed to the so-called legit site, knowing what to look for. That makes it very difficult to discover the real sites behind."

Dmitri clicked on a picture of two girls on a swing set. A completely different web site emerged on the screen.

"In this case, this site provides information and access for pedophiles and sexual predators of young girls ranging from thirteen to sixteen. Depending on the site, these perverts can do everything from buying these girls outright to finding places near them where they can have sex with the girls. They can also arrange for a week with these girls at a secret pedophile resort. Some of these girls go for upwards of fifty grand. All financial transactions are done on these sites and the money usually ends up at Kharkiv Privat Bank in the Ukraine. I dug into the sites listed on the last screen and they all lead back to the *Mogilschiiki*."

"You can bet J Otis Weil is involved as well," Mack said.

Dmitri brought up a new screen with six mug shots in two rows. "These six people are high ranking *Mogilschiiki*."

Peter couldn't take his eyes off the screen. He walked over to get a closer look. "These are the bastards who killed my wife and son."

"The four men on the right are currently in Zürich as is J Otis Weil," Dmitri said.

"And they're not leaving," Peter said with certainty.

Dmitri brought up an organization chart on the screen. At the top of the chart was a headshot of the Russian President. One level below was J Otis Weil next to an empty box. Below the empty box was written: *Mogilschiiki Boss*. On the bottom of the chart was a row of smaller pictures identified by location: London, Germany, Saudi Arabia, Iran, Asia and United States.

"The reason I want you to see this chart is because I have been unable to discover the name of the person now running the *Mogilschiiki*. Since the suicide of Sergei Vukovic," Dmitri made air quotes with his fingers when he said suicide, "I have been unable to figure out who runs the organization."

"If Khandelwal did go rogue, maybe we pay him a visit and see what he has to say," Mack said. "Perhaps he could identify the new head of the *Mogilschiiki*?"

"I'll drive," Peter said.

"Hold on a second," Giuliani said. "Before you rush out and get yourselves killed, give me time to clear things with the Swiss authorities and arrange a SWAT team to back you up."

"As long as it doesn't take hours," Peter said. "I don't like the fact the *Mogils* are in Zürich."

Mack walked out into the warehouse and strolled around as he thought. He meandered back into the room and said to Peter, "Let's go check on Hilda and Vlad. We can wait in your office until we hear from Giuliani and Paletz."

Peter nodded as he pulled out his phone and called Hilda. He held the phone to his ear as it rang. After a dozen rings, he hung up with a worried look.

"Hilda's not answering. She always, I mean always, answers my calls."

$

# CHAPTER 26

The drive back to Peter's office in the bookstore was a quiet ride. Peter was worried about Hilda and Mack knew better than to distract him from his thoughts. He could not imagine what Peter would do if he lost his only remaining family.

Peter parked in the underground garage in the building next to the bookstore. Mack stayed a step behind him as they made their way to the back entrance up to the office.

As Mack stood back waiting for Peter to unlock the door, his phone rang. It was Ray Gunn calling.

Before Mack could say hello, Gunn's voice was coming through the phone. "Giuliani got me up to speed on where you are and I called to reinforce what Giuliani and Paletz want you to do. Wait until they have a SWAT team ready to back you up before you take on the *Mogils*. Don't put yourself out there without backup."

Mack followed Peter into the office and waited for him to close and lock the back door then slide the bookcase in front of it.

"I understand, Ray. We have no intention of taking on the *Mogils*. Not until we've had a chance to talk to Khandelwal. By that time, Giuliani and Paletz will have their team in place."

"Good. Call me if anything new develops."

Mack slid his phone back in his pocket as Peter walked out the office and checked the bookstore out front. On his return he shook his head, silently telling Mack that Hilda and Vlad were not out front.

Peter opened a side door leading to a set of steps. He climbed the steps and pushed his way through another door, closing it behind him.

Mack felt helpless standing in the middle of the office. He strolled over and sat in the chair facing Peter's desk. He crossed and uncrossed his legs.

A minute later, Peter hurried down the steps and

hustled to his desk. He fired up his computer.

"Any sign of Hilda?" Mack asked.

"No and I'm afraid she may have gone after J Otis Weil."

"You don't know that." Mack said.

Peter ignored him and began typing on his computer.

After the computer beeped twice, Mack asked, "What are you doing?"

"Hilda's in Herrliberg, near Khandelwal's house."

"How do you know that?"

"After what happened with my wife and son, I installed a tracking program on Hilda's phone." Peter opened his desk drawer, removed his gun and slid it into his waistband. "Let's go," he said.

"We agreed to wait until Giuliani arranged for SWAT to back us up."

"You can wait. I'm going to find Hilda."

"Wait up," Mack said. He thought about calling Ray Gunn then thought better of it. If he did call Gunn, Peter would take off without him. Mack hustled down the steps behind Peter.

Mack sat quietly in the car as Peter gripped the steering wheel with both hands and his eyes glued to the road. His body was rigid and his jaw locked tight.

Mack was not about to ask him what he was thinking.

As they left the Zürich city limits heading south, Mack realized they were coming up on Keller's house. Three police cars with flashing blue lights were parked in front of Keller's house with two wheels on the curb. An ambulance was parked next to the front entrance. Peter slowed the car as they drove past. Mack saw paramedics wheeling out a gurney. Stretched out on top of the gurney and covered in a white sheet was a dead body.

"*Mogils*? Mack asked.

Peter nodded as he sped up. He said, "I know the area Khandelwal lives and so does Hilda. It is very hilly and we can use a vantage point from above to see if we can spot her. The one thing we can't do is surprise her. We get the lay of the land and devise our approach."

Mack stared out the passenger window and thought about what he wanted to know from Khandelwal. He wasn't too worried about Hilda and Vlad. They were well trained and could take care of themselves.

When they came into the town of *Herrliberg*,

Peter said, "Khandelwal's house is up there on the left. It's one of the modern houses in that complex overlooking the lake."

Mack looked up at a four houses similar in design. All had a full wall of windows looking down on the lake and a large patio out front. A waist-high glass fence ringed the complex.

Peter turned left off the main road and drove up a winding two-lane road with a 30 kilometer per hour (20 mph) speed limit. He kept to the speed limit as they climbed and drove past the houses. "That's his house, the last one down on the right."

Peter drove further up the hill then turned left onto a dark street and pulled over. Every house on the quiet street had a stone fence blocking the view of the street.

As soon as they were out of the car, Peter said, "We can get a good vantage point from back across the street. I saw an empty lot with no lights. Perfect place for surveillance."

Peter turned and faced Mack, "Do you have the weapon I gave you?"

Mack pulled the Colt .45 from his waistband behind his back and held it up.

Avoiding the corner streetlight, Peter approached the empty lot slowly and methodically.

At the near corner, Peter threw his left arm out, stopping Mack.

"There's a man crouched down in the far corner with binoculars resting on the wooden fence. Stay here," he ordered. Peter didn't wait for a response and crept along the back of the lot, staying in the darkness.

Mack focused on the crouching silhouette. Peter silently snuck up on the man. He was ten feet behind him when the man swung around with a handgun in his right hand. Mack held his breath watching Peter stand motionless.

Peter shook his finger at the man holding the gun.

It took Mack a few seconds to realize the shadow of a man pointing the gun at Peter was Vlad.

Mack waited until Peter waved him over.


Mack walked hesitantly over the uneven grass field, his eyes stealing glances down at Khandelwal's house a hundred yards below.

Peter waved more aggressively and Mack sped up, race walking the last fifty feet.

"What's going on?" Mack asked. "Where's Hilda?"

Vlad flicked his head toward Khandelwal's house. "She is down at house."

Peter took the binoculars from Vlad's hand and peered down at the house. He slowly swept the binoculars over every inch of the house. "I can't see her. I don't see anybody," he said and handed the binoculars to Mack.

"When we get here, we see three *Mogils* guarding house," Vlad said. "Little bit later, we see a man with no hair walk in with woman and J Otis Weil. Hilda go crazy when she see J Otis."

"How long ago was that?" Mack asked.

"Thirty minutes, I think. I tell Hilda wait until we have plan and more peoples. But, she not wait and go. I try stop her but she not listen."

Mack peered down at the house. "There is nobody outside the house now."

"Hilda get man at front door to come to her in street. She put gun in man's chest, hit him in head with metal bar then tie him up, gag him and drag him to hill. She push him with foot and he roll down hill. Little time later two *Mogils* on other side of house disappear but I not see how and I not see Hilda no more."

"Metal bar?" Mack looked puzzled. "Wouldn't the *Mogil* see that?"

Vlad shook his head. "Is expanding baton and very good for close fighting."

"Damn," Peter said. "When Hilda sets her mind to something, nothing gets in her way."

"What we do?" Vlad asked.

"We go down there, see what's going on and get my daughter."

"Shouldn't we wait for the backup?" Mack asked.

"We don't have time. The *Mogils* don't ask questions, they just shoot and kill."

Mack lifted the binoculars and looked back down at the house.

After a short pause, he said, "I have an idea."

$

# CHAPTER 27

As soon as Mack finished outlining his plan, Peter shook his head vehemently. "It's too easy, too simple. Besides, there is a ninety percent chance someone will put a bullet in you before you get inside the house."

Mack dismissed Peter's warning. "J Otis and his accomplice are inside. They won't let the *Mogils* shoot me until they know what I know. I may get tortured but if my plan works, you will be inside before that happens."

"Simple usually is best," Vlad said. "They not

expect direct approach. Mack only has to take their attention away from the perimeter for short while. There are three of us and five them. It won't be fair fight. We won't even need minute."

Peter saw blood seeping through Vlad's pant leg. He looked at him with concern. "Vlad," Peter said, "you have a bum leg so you're not one hundred percent."

"Even with my leg, I better than *Mogils*." Vlad jumped up and landed on his injured leg. "See."

"This is no time for heroics. Hilda's life may be on the line," Mack said.

"I am best." Vlad grinned. He took the binoculars from Mack and studied the house.

"We go now. He handed the binoculars back to Mack. Give us right time to get in positions."

"Billy, give your gun to Vlad. You don't want that on you when you're inside. It's imperative to look like you're not a threat."

Mack gave the gun to Vlad handle first. Vlad walked to the street, trying to hide his limp.

Peter reached into his sport coat pocket and handed Mack a wire with a metal loop on each end.

"What's this?" Mack asked.

"It's a garrote. From behind you wrap it around the neck, press your leg against the back and pull. It crushes the larynx and silently kills."

"What if they pat me down?"

"If you get patted down, it will be for guns and knives." Peter said and started to walk away.

Mack shoved the G-knot in his pocket. "When will I have the chance to use this?"

"You may or may not have a chance. The only possible time is if Vlad and I take the attention off you." Peter said. "Better to have something, just in case."

"I wait five minutes, no more no less," Mack said louder than he wanted.

Peter held his right hand above his shoulder with his five fingers spread wide.

As soon as Peter and Vlad were out of sight, Mack looked at his watch. As the seconds ticked by, he tried to convince himself everything would go smoothly. Each time however, doubt seeped into his mind, he thought of Siva and whispered, "I gotta do what I gotta do."

After the longest five minutes of his life, he spotted Vlad standing by the side of the house. Mack marched over to the street and headed down the hill. As he approached the house, his pace slowed. A four-foot stone wall ringed Khandelwal's yard. There was an arched opening leading to the front door.

The walls of Khandelwal's house were smooth concrete painted white. There were two long narrow windows running vertically along each side of the steel front door. The blinds inside both windows were closed.

Mack shook the fear from his mind and strolled up to the front door. He steadied himself with a deep breath then pounded on the door three times. He inadvertently took a half step back.

He felt like someone was watching him. He looked around for a camera but didn't find one.

The front door swung open. Standing in the doorway was a woman with black pistol in her hand and pointed at Mack. He looked over her shoulder inside the house to see J Otis Weil strutting across the room.

"What the hell," she said. "Giuliani just told me you were dead." She composed herself and put the pistol against Mack's chest. "Where's my money?"

"I'll talk to your boss?"

"I'm in charge."

Mack recalled the picture hanging in Gullberg's apartment. Her eyes in the picture didn't have the venom they have now. He quickly said, "Let's make a deal. I know where your money is and I'm the only person who can get back. If you want to shoot me go ahead. When the Russian President finds out, well, that would give him a hundred million reasons to kill you." Mack raised his chin toward the room inside and yelled, "Isn't that right, J Otis?"

Geissel turned to look back and Mack snatched the pistol by the barrel, twisted it and jerked it from her hand.

Mack flicked the pistol toward the room. "Deal's off. Let's go say hi to your boss."

Mack stayed close behind Geissel with the pistol a few inches behind her head. "Siva's alive, in case you were concerned." He tapped the back of her head with the barrel. "You won't be if you even breathe wrong."

When they entered the living room, Mack gripped Geissel's hair and pulled her to a stop.

He looked over to his left to find Lee Khandelwal tied to a chair, blood flowing from his nose, lip and right cheek. His eyes were swollen nearly shut and the skin around both was the color of red wine. His right thigh was bleeding from a bullet hole and his left hand was wrapped in a blood-soaked towel.

On the floor, a few yards to Khandelwal's left lay Marek Gullberg, a pool of blood around his head. Mack counted two bullet holes in Gullberg's forehead.

J Otis strolled toward Mack and stopped when he noticed the gun in his hand. J Otis was short and thin with round wire rim glasses resting on his nose. He wore a tailored blue blazer with gray slacks and a white dress shirt, no tie. His black shoes had one-inch high heels and clicked when he walked, like a tap dancer. Sewn into the top of his head were multiple rows of hair plugs. The scalp between the rows glistened from the ceiling lights.

"Billy Mack as I live and breath. I always knew you were stupid but to stroll in here with all my people around makes you the dumbest asshole I've ever known. When will you learn?" J Otis raised his hand and a plain-looking woman emerged from the side of the room, an automatic pistol in her hand. "Meet Bella, she takes care of problems for me, even small problems like you. Let me give you some advice Mack. Put the gun down and I may let you live for a little while anyway," J Otis said.

Mack jammed the pistol against the back of Geissel's head. "Tell Jez-A-Bella over there to put her gun down and I won't splatter your girlfriend's brains all over you."

J Otis laughed hauntingly. "I don't give a damn what you do with her. She doesn't mean shit to me." He smiled cruelly. "I've outgrown her. Or, I should say, she's outgrown me."

Mack felt a heavy weight hit his chest and slide down his body as Geissel fainted and fell back into him. She landed at his feet. With Geissel on the ground Mack lost his cover.

"You're a fucking loser, Mack. Put the gun down now." J Otis smiled victoriously.

Mack looked over to see Bella aiming her pistol at him. He slowly bent down and placed the pistol on the stone floor.

As soon as he released the gun, Geissel snatched the gun off the floor and jumped to her feet. She laughed as she walked over and handed the piece to J Otis.

J Otis turned to Bella, her automatic still pointed at Mack's forehead. "You know I didn't mean what I said about your sister."

Bella kept her gun pointed at Mack, her face emotionless.

J Otis said, "Go check the area Bella and make sure this idiot came alone."

Mack watched Bella march outside, turn left and

walk to the dark end of the patio. When he turned his eyes back into the room, Geissel was standing directly in front of Khandelwal. She had a surgical scalpel in her hand and a demented look on her face.

In a shrill voice she said, "Where is our money?"

Khandelwal raised his chin in defiance then clenched his jaw in anticipation of another finger being cut off.

"He doesn't know where it is," Mack yelled, scaring Geissel. "I told you that I'm the one who reversed the wire transfers, not him." Mack waited for Geissel to move the scalpel away from Khandelwal. "The money never made it to your bank in Kharkiv. It was returned to the bank in Miami and I directed it to then be sent to a numbered account back here in Zürich. I've also notified the authorities of who actually owns the money."

Mack turned his gaze to J Otis. "That's what us dumb assholes do, J Otis."

Watching J Otis fume, Mack added, "Oh, and your private plane has been grounded. There is no way you are leaving Switzerland." Mack said it such conviction that he even believed his own words.

J Otis aimed the pistol at Mack, his hand shaking.

Mack held his hand up. "Maybe I will let you fly

back to Russia. The President will understand you losing his money as well as exposing his sex trafficking connection to the *Mogilschiiki*, which is being shut down as we speak. You think he'll pin a medal on your chest when he learns you cut off a large part of his income?"

A commotion at the patio door grabbed Mack's attention. Bella had a grip on Peter's ponytail as she pushed him into the room.

Peter struggled to loosen Bella's grip then relaxed and gave a nearly imperceptible wink to Mack.

Mercy Geissel squealed as she ran to J Otis and tried to pull the pistol from his hand.

J Otis shoved her away. "What the hell are you doing?"

Geissel shrieked and wheezed as she failed to suck in enough oxygen. She was hyperventilating. She lowered her head and dropped her hands to her knees as she struggled to breathe.

J Otis grinned widely as he rubbed her back. "See, I told you I knew where he was. Never doubt me again."

Geissel slowly regained her breathing. She straightened up and let out a long tired breath. "I never thought it was possible."

"He's all yours," J Otis said proudly.

Geissel walked over to Peter. She stood close and sniffed. "I want to smell the pig who killed our parents in cold blood." She slapped Peter across the face with every ounce of strength she possessed.

Peter didn't flinch. His eyes bore into Geissel's. "You're parents were the pigs. They bought and sold young girls into prostitution, girls as young as twelve and thirteen."

Geissel slapped him hard again.

"I didn't kill them in cold blood. Your father tried to shoot me but he was too much of a loser. Your mother, she was the brains behind it all. She came at me with a knife. At least she had the stones to come at me. I admired that in her before I shot her."

Geissel grabbed Peter by the crotch. "You're not going to die quickly like my parents. You will suffer until you've paid the appropriate price. After that, I will hunt down your daughter and do the same thing to her." Geissel laughed chillingly.

"No need to hunt for his daughter," Hilda said as she walked in off the patio. She fired twice in rapid succession hitting Bella in the temple both times.

Bella crumbled to the floor.

Geissel sprinted over and reached for the automatic pistol in Bella's limp hand.

Hilda fired again, hitting the pistol and spinning it across the floor.

J Otis moved like a cat and was behind Mack with his pistol stuck in Mack's back. "Go get the gun, Mercy and follow me. I am walking out of here with Billy Mack. If anyone even flinches, Mack is dead." J Otis grabbed Mack by the back of the shirt and backed out of the room.

Geissel picked up Bella's pistol and pointed it at Peter. She grinned at Hilda.

"Looks like you have a decision to make," Hilda said. "You can fire but it'll be the last thing you ever do. Go ahead, there's a high probability you won't kill him. I, on the other hand, will not miss. If you don't believe me, take look at your friend."

Geissel looked down at Bella on the floor, her left leg jerking impulsively. "That's my sister."

Before backing out of the room, Geissel pointed at Peter, her voice soaked in venom. "I will kill your little bitch daughter in front of you before I kill you. Watch your backs. I know who you are now."

"Get the door, Mercy," J Otis ordered. He pulled hard on Mack's shirt and jerked him backward.

Three loud knocks at the front door caused J Otis to turn. He said, "Kill whoever is at the door, Mercy."

Hilda caught eyes with Peter and mouthed, "Vlad."

Geissel readied the automatic pistol then flung the door open.

No one was standing in the doorway. Geissel cautiously stepped out, looked left then right. She turned back to J Otis. "There's nobody here."

J Otis pulled Mack outside and slammed the front door shut. He said, "Lead the way, Mercy. I have car parked down the street."

Vlad stepped around the corner of the house, staying in the darkness. "Let Billy go, J Otis or I kill you and your little friend."

Recognizing the voice, J Otis laughed then said, "You teamed up with Vlad the Impaler, Mack? You *are* stupid. When he worked for me, he never did anything right."

Mack squirmed hoping to divert J Otis' attention.

Instead, J Otis stuck his gun against Mack's temple. "There's two of us Vlad and one of you."

"That make it not a fair fight," Vlad said. "You

must get more peoples."

Vlad fired, hitting Geissel in the right shoulder. She spun around, flinging the automatic pistol across the yard.

Mack had no time to think. He whirled around whipping his elbow and knocking away J Otis' hand holding the gun.

J Otis fired barely missing Mack's head.

The blast from the gunshot pierced Mack's eardrum. The fierce explosion echoed through his body.

J Otis sprinted to the street and around the stone fence. He ducked below the wall so only his hair plugs were visible as he ran away.

Vlad fired a volley of shots at J Otis, his bullets ricocheting off the top of the stone wall.

Mack walked over to Geissel lying on the ground squirming in pain and frantically searching for her gun. She didn't see Mack walk up on her.

Mack turned her on her stomach and pulled her arms behind her back. Vlad tossed him a zip tie as he hurried past. Mack secured Geissel's wrists together then marched out to the street and stood next to Vlad.

Mack looked down the street to see J Otis

jumping into the back seat of a Range Rover.

Vlad aimed and fired, shattering the back window. The Range Rover squealed away.

Mack and Vlad and watched the brake lights of the Range Rover disappear down the hill and around a bend.

A few seconds later, headlights came around the corner and sped up the hill toward them.

Vlad and Mack walked back behind the stone wall and waited for the car to pull up and stop on the street in front of them.

Both front doors of the car flew open. Giuliani stepped from the driver's seat and Paletz jumped out of the passenger's side.

"What the hell's going on?" Paletz demanded.

Geissel crawled to her feet and started to run.

Hilda stepped out from the front door and fired a shot over Geissel's head. "The next shot won't miss," she yelled. Geissel stopped in her tracks, spun around and spit on the ground. "You should have killed me."

Hilda smiled as she walked up to Mack and Vlad. She looked around and her smile disappeared. "Where is J Otis Weil?"

"He got away," Mack replied. "I should say ran away. But don't worry, J Otis will rear his ugly head again."

Peter strolled out and stopped when he saw Giuliani and Paletz staring at him, still in disbelief.

"Tom Garrahan does it again," Guiliani said. "Jesus H. Christ, Tom do you ever follow orders."

"You must have me confused with someone named Tom Garrahan who looks like me," Peter said and walked back inside.

Giuliani smiled at Hilda. "You and your dad were ordered to wait until we arrived. We have special ops team on the way."

"They're no longer needed," Hilda said. Vlad took her by the arm and walked her back inside.

"We know who stole your money," Mack said. He pointed at Geissel. "Other than J Otis Weil, I haven't figured out if she was working with anyone else, perhaps Gullberg. Unfortunately, the dead woman inside put two in his head. If he was involved, it's obvious he was expendable."

"Damn it," Paletz said as he shook his head in disgust. "Gullberg was an informant for us. He fed us valuable information on Mideast money financing our enemies as well as terrorist bent of destroying Israel. He was a hero to our people." Paletz nodded sadly, "He will get a state burial in Israel."

Mack said, "When the special ops team gets here, they will find three *Mogilschiiki* out back. One of them is somewhere down the hill. You don't want them here when the Swiss cops arrive. Also, Lee Khandelwal is inside, badly beaten, a bullet hole in his leg and missing a finger. He's in bad shape and needs a doctor."

Giuliani pulled out his phone, tapped the screen three times and brought it to his ear.

"Who you calling?" Mack asked.

"I'm calling a discreet ambulance we use in situations like this."

"Situations like this?" Mack asked.

"On the way here, I learned Khandelwal is one of our high level, deep cover agents. I trained with him at the Farm before he mysteriously left. I can't have an agent dying on my watch now can I?"

"What about Siva?"

"Ray Gunn has the top doctors from the Mayo Clinic flying into Zürich."

$

# EPILOGUE

Two days later, Peter, Hilda and Vlad walked into the Safari bar and peered around like it was their first time there. Sitting on the same stool at the bar facing the door was the same old man nursing a glass of beer with an unlit cigarette stuck between his fingers. He smiled at Hilda. Both front teeth were still missing.

Vlad ordered a bottle of Purity vodka from the bartender while Peter and Hilda walked over to Mack's table.

Peter clamped his hand on Mack's shoulder.

"Dmitri hacked into the Miami bank and transferred the money back to Siva's account at Keller Bank. He drafted a report detailing the timeline to prove that Siva never instructed the bank to transfer out the money. Everyone knows she was never involved. Ray Gunn made sure of it."

"It makes me rethink keeping my money in a bank," Hilda said.

"Dmitri has special skills and the most sophisticated intelligence agency behind him." Peter hesitated so he could watch Hilda's face. When he didn't get the response he wanted, he said, "The CIA and Mossad probably have agents planted inside Keller Bank who provided codes for his access. That's a long way of saying banks are safe."

Mack's mind flash-backed to Khandelwal tied to his chair, beaten, shot and missing a finger. "If that's true, I wonder who the agent is inside Keller Bank?" he said.

"We may never know," Hilda said, mockingly. "My guess is Khandelwal and Gullberg."

Peter smiled proudly at his daughter.

"What if Khandelwal did go rogue and was working with Geissel before betraying her and J Otis?" Mack asked, stirring the pot.

Peter shrugged. "They wouldn't torture him. If

Khandelwal stole the money, he would have been dead before we got there."

Hilda stood as Vlad approached holding a tall, thin bottle in one hand and four glasses in the other. She took the glasses and set them on the table.

Vlad poured vodka into each glass then raised his glass. "We do good and not be killed." A wide grin grew across his face. He said, "*Vashe zrodovye*. That mean 'to your health.'" Vlad downed his glass.

Not to be outdone by Vlad, Hilda said, "Here's lookin' up your old address." She downed her glass and mimicked a kiss to Vlad.

Mack and Peter silently raised their glasses and took a sip.

"What did Dmitri find out?" Mack asked Peter.

"A person with total access to the bank's system erased the original transactions and substituted the actual wire transfers and security protocols with doctored data showing Siva as the person initiating the transaction exactly as the bank's security required. Dmitri is still working to identify that person."

"Dollar to a dime it was Mercedes Geissel."

"No more shop talk," Hilda said. She turned and faced Mack. "Did you stop by and see Siva?"

"Not yet. I spoke to her doctor this morning. She's recovering from the surgery she had yesterday and can't be disturbed. I'm going over later today to check. The doctors from the Mayo Clinic should know more by then."

"Do you want company?"

"Sure but I don't know if she'll even know we're there."

At the hospital, a team of doctors in white coats stood in Siva's room conversing in hushed tones while a nurse checked Siva's vitals.

Ray Gunn sat near the head of the bed listening to the doctors. Seeing Mack out in the hall brought a somber smile to his face. He excused himself, patted Siva's hand then rubbed his baldhead as he strolled out of the room.

"Let's go into the visitor's lounge," Gunn said.

"What's the latest on Siva?" Mack asked.

"When the doctors finish examining her, they'll let us know."

"When can we see her?" Hilda asked.

"Once the doctor's determine her course of treatment."

"What do you know so far?" Peter asked.

"She's tough and a real fighter. She's lucky to be alive and will need at least one more surgery. Unfortunately the doctor's must wait until her infection is gone, probably another a day or two before they can operate again."

Gunn marched over to the corner of the visitor's lounge and gestured for everyone to sit.

Vlad limped over to a small sofa with his arm around Hilda's shoulders. She helped him sit and adjust his injured leg.

"How's the leg?" Gunn asked. "Do you want the doctors to take a look at it?"

Vlad shook his head. "It is stiff and sore, but I am to be good."

Hilda stroked Vlad's arm. "When we're done here, one of the doctors will examine your leg."

Vlad opened his mouth to object when Mack cut him off.

"Don't argue. You'll never win. Trust me."

Peter deftly changed the subject. "Has Mercedes Geissel talked yet?"

Gunn slowly nodded. "She was immediately whisked off from Khandelwal's house to a rendition center in Orosháza, Hungary. She was tight-lipped until she saw the high walls of the old prison. Once inside she quickly gave everything up."

"She is at old Soviet prison there?" Vlad asked. "Is not closed?"

"It's a rendition site now."

Peter shot Gunn a funny look. "It's not one of ours, is it?"

"No, it's not. Orosháza was a secret Soviet prison still in use years after the Berlin Wall fell because top Hungarian political leaders and former communists were paid off by the Russians to secretly run the prison until the Russians could quietly extract the remains of the bodies buried in the prison cemetery. Basically, Russia was determined to hide the evidence of political prisoners, mostly Jewish, sent to die in Orosháza. The Israelis learned of this and blackmailed Hungary to hand over control of the prison."

"If the Israelis have her, she won't breathe free air for a long time," Peter said.

"Did she say who took the money and why?" Mack asked.

"A mole inside the CIA passed on information to Russia that an account was being set up to finance unrest in Russia as payback for meddling in our elections. Geissel claimed not to know the name of the mole. She was contacted by J Otis at the direction of the Russian President and offered two million dollars to pilfer the account. When J Otis learned Siva was involved, he came up with the plan to pin the theft on Siva figuring Billy would get involved."

"Sounds like J Otis," Mack said. "Why did Geissel agree? She didn't need the money."

"Geissel turned down the money but agreed with two conditions. First, J Otis and the Russians had to find the man that killed her parents. The other condition was to give the *Mogils* ten million of the stolen money."

"Why the *Mogils*?" Mack asked.

"Geissel and her sister, Bella, ran the *Mogils* after Vukovic committed *suicide*." Gunn smiled widely at the ruse. "The sisters were tired of being patient waiting for Vukovic to find Peter. So they took matters into their own hands. Geissel sent Bella to Kiev to eliminate Vukovic."

"If Geissel was involved with the *Mogils*, how did she end up at Keller Bank?" Mack asked.

"Keller had penchant for teenage girls. Because of his position as a leading private banker, he kept his obsession to girls older than sixteen. He went on the dark web and chose Mercedes Geissel who'd lied about her age. He took her and her sister in with one intention in mind." Gunn flicked his eyebrows up. "Geissel had her plan to find the killer of her parents and acquiesced to Keller's advances but Bella vowed to kill him if he ever touched her. She scared the hell out of him. With Mercedes, he quickly learned she had a sharp mind and business savvy. He had no heirs so she became his de facto successor at the bank. Once inside the bank she was contacted by Vukovic to launder *Mogil* money. She and Bella kept to their plan and waited."

"Those are two sick girls," Hilda said.

You have to remember," Gunn said, Mercy saw her parents be killed and Bella saw the hole in her father's head as he lay next to her dead mother. That'll fuck you up."

"Why kill Siva and Billy? Peter asked. Pinning the theft of the money on them I understand."

"They had to eliminate Siva and Billy to keep anyone from digging into the evidence and finding the truth. With them dead, no one would suspect Geissel and J Otis. They would presume someone inside the intel agencies killed Billy and Siva to cover agency involvement."

Hilda shook her head in disgust. "What do you think will happen to Beat Keller and his bank?"

"Keller's dead," Gunn said flatly. "Bella put two

in his forehead."

"How do they know Bella killed him?"

"Geissel gave her up. Since Bella was dead, Geissel had no problem pinning Keller's murder on her. She claimed she ordered Bella to leave Keller alone."

"Self preservation," Mack said.

"And the bank?" Hilda asked.

"The bank will be secretly owned by the CIA and Mossad through a trust. Lee Khandelwal will take over once he's healed. It's a great cover for the CIA and Mossad to track illegal businesses using the bank. It will also help fund their covert operations and let them avoid going to their governments to ask for black ops money."

Mack looked at Gunn and asked. "Once Mossad extracts everything out of Geissel, what's in store for her?"

Gunn answered, "She will be taken to Israel and charged with the murder of Marek Gullberg. Her confession is already written and her plea bargain agreeing to life in prison has been signed. Paletz will show her the documents she signed once she gets to Israel."

$ $ $

# ABOUT THE AUTHOR

Johnny Mee has authored 4 other Billy Mack Thrillers.
Check out his web site at johnnynovels.com

59444566R00162

Made in the USA
Columbia, SC
03 June 2019